SNOW ANGEL

Snow Angel

Copyright © 2023 by Gary J. Rose. All rights reserved.

No part of this publication may be reproduced, stored in a retrieval system, or transmitted in any form or by any means, digital, electronic, mechanical, photocopying, recording, or otherwise, or conveyed via the Internet or a website without prior written permission of the publisher, except in the case of brief quotations embodied in critical articles and reviews.

This is a work of fiction. Names, characters, places, and incidents are products of the author's imagination or have been used fictitiously and are not to be construed as real. Any resemblance to persons, living or dead, actual events, locales, or organizations is coincidental.

ISBN: 979-8-9886823-5-6 (hardback)
979-8-9886823-6-3 (paperback)

Printed in the United States of America

SNOW ANGEL

A Jeannie Loomis Novel

GARY J. ROSE

DEDICATION

As I pen the final words of *Snow Angel* and prepare to share it with the world, one crucial aspect demands recognition before its publication – the book dedication. In this moment, I, the (in)famous writer, endeavor to captivate the hearts of potential readers, for within these pages lies the eleventh thrilling adventure of Jeannie Loomis.

To all those who have embarked on this journey with Jeannie from the very beginning and have continued to be ardent fans through twelve novels, I extend my sincerest gratitude. Your unwavering support fuels my creative drive, and I hope *Snow Angel* only strengthens our bond.

First and foremost, a special appreciation goes to my sister, Debbie (Rose) Miller. Once again, she selflessly immersed herself in the manuscript, diligently catching errors and offering invaluable suggestions. Her dedication to perfection has made *Snow Angel* shine brightly.

I must also express a heartfelt thank you to Gillian McDonald, whose editing prowess continues to astound me. Her longstanding connection with

Jeannie's world and her unwavering curiosity about her exploits always lead to the question, "What is Jeannie up to now?" Gillian's expert touch elevates my writing to heights I could never attain alone.

To both Debbie and Gillian, your contributions have imprinted on these pages, and your support has propelled this novel to new heights. Your belief in my work has been an inspiration, and I am forever grateful.

And lastly, to the readers who breathe life into the stories I create, your enthusiasm and love for Jeannie's adventures drive me to keep writing. Without you, these tales would merely be words on paper, lacking the magic that comes from being embraced by dedicated readers like yourselves.

So, with immense appreciation and unwavering affection, I dedicate *Snow Angel* to my sister, Debbie (Rose) Miller, and Gillian McDonald – two incredible souls who have left an indelible mark on this book. And to every reader who opens these pages, know that it is your spirit that brings the characters to life and imbues the narrative with its true magic.

Thank you all for being a part of this extraordinary journey.

A HEARTFELT EXPRESSION OF GRATITUDE FROM THE AUTHOR

First, I want to express my sincere gratitude for choosing to read my Jeannie Loomis novel. Whether this is your first encounter with Jeannie or you have followed her thrilling adventures before, I hope you thoroughly enjoy this latest installment.

In this gripping tale, Jeannie finds herself separated from her team as she joins forces with the Idaho State Police to investigate a notorious serial killer known as the Snow Angel. This book marks the eleventh novel in the Jeannie Loomis series. If you find yourself captivated by the story, I kindly ask that you consider leaving a review on Amazon.com and sharing your experience with others. Additionally, I'm thrilled to share that some of my novels are currently being considered for feature film adaptations.

Many of my fans often inquire about my favorite authors, and while I admire several talented writers, three immediately spring to mind. John Stanford, renowned for his Lucas Davenport Prey novel series, has significantly influenced my protagonist, as you may notice some shared attributes between Lucas Davenport and Jeannie Loomis.

James Patterson holds a special place among my favorite authors, and I find his enthralling Alex Cross novels truly captivating. The character of Alex Cross, with his background as a psychologist, brings a distinct advantage to his investigative prowess.

Similarly, Jeannie Loomis, the protagonist in my novels, shares this advantage as she also possesses a Ph.D. in Psychology. This psychological expertise grants Jeannie a valuable edge during her own investigations. Drawing inspiration from Dr. Cross, Jeannie skillfully utilizes her understanding of the human mind to analyze suspects, decipher motives, and navigate intricate webs of clues.

The incorporation of this psychological dimension adds depth and complexity to Jeannie's character, enriching the thrill and suspense of her stories. It's remarkable how authors like James Patterson and the qualities of their iconic protagonists can influence and shape the development of characters in other literary works, such as Jeannie Loomis.

Lee Child's Reacher series has been a significant source of inspiration for me, greatly influencing my writing style. Regrettably, Lee Child recently made an announcement that he will cease writing any further Jack Reacher novels. Citing the reason that he felt he was "aging out" of being able to continue producing books featuring the beloved character, Child's decision marks a significant turning point in his literary career.

The news saddened many fans, including yours truly, who have come to appreciate and cherish the thrilling adventures of Jack Reacher. However, it is not uncommon for authors to embark on new creative paths or explore fresh avenues to challenge themselves.

Lee Child's remarkable contribution to the world of literature through the Reacher series will undoubtedly leave a lasting legacy, and his decision opens up opportunities for both him and his readers to embark on new and exciting literary journeys.

Furthermore, I'm proud to mention that four of the Jeannie Loomis novels are partially inspired by historical events. The thrilling tales of *Ark of the Covenant-Raid on the Church of Our Lady Mary of Zion*, *House of Special Purpose*, *The Fourth Reich*, and *The Phantom Train* delve into captivating historical backdrops. Notably, *Ark of the Covenant* and *The Fourth Reich* have been particularly well-received by readers, emerging as two of my best-selling works.

I sincerely appreciate your decision to choose *Snow Angel*. Thank you for giving it a chance, and I genuinely hope that you thoroughly enjoy your reading experience.

Gary J. Rose

WHO IS FBI AGENT JEANNIE LOOMIS?

Jeannie Loomis is a committed yet imperfect agent in her forties working within the FBI. Her journey through the ranks took place during a time when the upper echelons of the bureau were predominantly male-dominated. Raised by deeply religious parents with a strong sense of patriotism, she continues to attend mass every weekend as a reminder of her upbringing.

Following the passing of her adoptive parents, Jeannie's pursuit of excellence propelled her to the role of Assistant Special Agent in Charge at the San Francisco FBI office. Her shielding from the agency's intricate politics is owed to her capable supervisor, Lomax, who holds the position of Special Agent in Charge.

Enduring the collapse of two marriages due to the strains of her demanding job, Jeannie found herself spiraling into a cycle of frequenting bars, often succumbing to heavy drinking and waking up beside unfamiliar partners. A tragic incident resulted in her pregnancy, which tragically ended in a violent confrontation at the substation where she was stationed.

Armed with a Ph.D. in psychology, Jeannie, along with her closest confidant and partner, Ismail Flores, has been instrumental in a series of high-profile investigations, some of which remained concealed from public knowledge due to their sensitive nature. Uncovering the truth about her biological heritage following her birth mother's demise revealed a startling secret: Jeannie is a wealthy heir, a revelation she only recently disclosed to Flores.

Much like the famed fictional investigator Lucas Davenport popularized by author John Stanford, Jeannie subscribes to the belief that achieving the greater good sometimes necessitates morally complex methods.

A snow angel is a
simple depression in
snow in the shape
of an angel

CHAPTER 1

Gabriel sat behind the wheel of his eighteen-wheeler as he cruised down the double-lane highway while listening to a conservative talk radio station. The host's words resonated with him, and he found himself nodding in agreement as heavy snow flurries began to land on his windshield.

Like the sentiments shared by numerous individuals who were calling the show, he believed that one of the critical issues plaguing our society was the gradual infiltration of criminals into state legislatures, Congress, and even the presidency. To rectify this situation, he strongly advocated for states to convene a Constitutional Convention as outlined in Article 5 of the Constitution. In his view, this was the only viable solution to address the problem. Without such measures, he was concerned that the nation might face the risk of another civil war.

The highway road crew had piled up snowbanks on both sides of the road, and the asphalt was gradually disappearing. Gabriel hoped he could reach his destination without having to put on snow chains.

As a former Green Beret from the Vietnam era, Gabriel considered himself a Constitutional Republican, proud of his political beliefs. He had staunchly supported the former president and firmly believed that the last election had been rigged by the Democrats. In his mind, he longed for a return to in-person voting with photo identification requirements, voting on the day of the election, and immediate public posting of the results.

Becoming an independent trucker had been a choice Gabriel made to earn extra money for himself and his wife. They enjoyed monthly visits to the local Indian casino, and the additional income came in handy, especially after buying Christmas presents for their family and friends. Gabriel relied on his veteran's pension, retirement from the Teamsters, and Social Security, but some months were tight.

He managed his high blood pressure, taking a pill each night, but he thanked God he was still in relatively good shape. At 6'1" and 200 lbs with a full head of hair, he felt fortunate. The bone-on-bone arthritis in his knees bothered him, but he opted for cortisone shots instead of knee replacements. Tonight, despite a recent shot, his right leg was niggling him due to the long haul and the cold weather, even with the cab heater set to maximum.

Suddenly, everything changed in an instant, and Gabriel almost lost control of his rig. Reacting quickly, he pulled the trailer brake lever, avoiding the foot brakes to prevent a jackknife. It felt like an eternity, but he managed to bring the truck to a stop. Switching on his emergency flashers, he maneuvered his truck as far off the road as possible next to a towering snowbank. Climbing down from the cab with a flashlight, he walked cautiously toward the spot where he had seen something.

There she lay, resembling a snow angel, he thought. She was as white as the snow, dressed only in a Christmas sweater and black panties. Her hands were tied and stretched out above her head, with the other end of the rope wrapped around her neck. Her blonde hair fanned out around her head, resembling a halo, like a snow angel.

She appeared to be a teenager or maybe a college student. Gabriel did not approach the body; he knew the signs of death and didn't want to disturb the scene. He reached for his cell phone and dialed 9-1-1. He retrieved the emergency triangles from his truck, placed them on the roadway, and waited for the first responders to arrive. Damn, he had been making good time.

Within ten minutes, an Idaho State Police Officer arrived at the scene, quickly joined by several others, including detectives. Gabriel provided his statement and was eventually released, grateful that the snow had let up and he could continue his run.

Officer Stewart, a twelve-year veteran, chose not to approach the body directly but instead cordoned the area off with police tape. Even from a distance, he could see the vacant stare on her face. Glancing at the snow around the body, he noticed the absence of footprints, suggesting that either she had been dumped there or recent snowfall had covered the perpetrator's tracks.

Detectives Max Elders and Alex Gordon arrived a short time later and took over. They climbed the snowbank, maintaining a distance of eight feet from the body. There was nothing more they could do until the coroner arrived. Elders was more senior than his partner, Gordon, having transferred in from the LAPD three years prior to Gordon's hiring.

The two escaped being assigned to the Idaho quadruple college student murders in Moscow. With rumors even inside the Moscow Police Department of a cluster-fuck and parents and the media demanding answers, they were glad they were held in reserve by their supervisor in case another major investigation sprang up. Sure enough, here they were, freezing their asses off, waiting for the coroner.

A little over an hour later, Doctor Judy Alshire arrived with two assistants. "So, gentlemen, what, pray tell, do we have tonight?"

"Well, the reporting party, a trucker, discovered what he believed to be a snow angel," Morris said, aiming his flashlight at the corpse in the snow.

The state's forensic team arrived a few minutes later and was requested to put up some lights to illuminate the area before Dr. Alshire climbed up to the snow mound. Gordon had to help her up the snowpack as she also noted the absence of footprints. "Do we know when the last heavy snowfall happened?" she asked.

"About five hours ago," Elders replied, "but we aren't sure about the amount of snow."

Dr. Alshire called her two assistants over requesting that they bring up a shovel in addition to the body bag. Gordon again helped the two coroner's assistants, Tommy Underwood and Laura Lawson. Elders could tell by Gordon's approach to Lawson that he was a bit smitten by her, and why not? She was a striking lady with long black hair pulled back into a ponytail.

Remaining at the base of the snow mound, Gordon and Elders watched as the doctor scraped away a few inches of snow in the hope there might be some type of foot impression left behind, but there was none. She told her two assistants to remain with the body and, with the help of Morris again, climbed back down to the roadway, where she asked for a ladder from the forensic team. She climbed almost to the top rung of the ladder and continued to look at the body.

"Laura, get a tape measure out and see how deep the body is in the snow. Start at her head and then around the body." Laura gave each measurement to Tommy Underwood, who recorded it on a piece of paper attached to a clipboard.

By the time Laura was finished, Dr. Alshire had made it back up to the body. She looked at Laura's measurements and called down to Gordon and Morris to climb up the snowbank. "I will examine the body, but first, I wanted measurements to be taken to see if my theory holds water. She pointed to different areas of the corpse. "Here, at the head, if you notice, the body is approximately two inches into the snow. As we walk around the body, Laura's measurement shows a depth of approximately two to three inches, except for the torso and, obviously, her derriere.

"Meaning?" asked Gordon.

"You will need someone to do the math, but preliminarily, I think your snow angel was thrown from the cab of a truck.

"As she traveled through the air, her hair sprayed out like a halo, and her arms ended up in the position they are now in. Someone good at math should be able to determine the height of the cab and how close it was to the snowbank." She looked at the forensic team leader, gave him the measurements Laura had taken, and suggested how they should proceed in their investigation. She then turned to the body.

"Okay, let's see what we have here. I'm going to guess that she is in her early twenties." She looked at the forensic team leader. "You know, the snow is making this a lot more difficult. Why don't you take the pictures you need? Hopefully, you can do so without getting too close to the body."

The forensic team took several photos from different angles, including those areas where Dr. Alshire pointed to the depth of the body. Once they finished, Dr. Alshire continued her examination. "No purse or wallet and no cell phone unless those items were thrown out and are under the snow somewhere, although I doubt it." She looked back at the body.

"As I said, early twenties. Blond hair and looks like blue eyes. Strangulation marks on her neck from the rope. Let's bag her hands in case we get lucky with transfer DNA. I will determine later if she was a victim of sexual assault. I assume she was, but you know what they say about assuming anything. The rope on her arms was just wrapped around, probably put there after she died and before she was thrown." She looked at Tommy and Laura. "That's about all we can do here. Let's tag her and bag her. I will post her tomorrow morning. Does 10:00 hours work for you two? "We will be there," Elders replied.

CHAPTER 2

Jeannie glanced out the window of her cozy cabin and observed the snow falling heavily. The vibrant red hue of her Corvette remained hidden beneath the snowy layer that clung to its sleek fiberglass exterior. Sipping her tea, she yearned for the snowfall to cease, hoping for clear weather for the rest of the week. She knew that snow and Corvettes were not a good combination. Consulting the Internet, she discovered that the storm front would pass later that evening, bringing with it warmer temperatures. Relieved by this news, she added another log to the crackling fire and surveyed her expansive log cabin.

She had acquired the cabin a few years after her team's investigation into Frank Silva and his renegade group of ex-military personnel. Together with a female biblical professor, they believed they had pinpointed the exact location of the Ark of the Covenant and planned to steal it. Regrettably, the investigation had come to an abrupt halt, leaving no trace of the suspects. It was as if they had vanished into thin air. The entire ordeal continued to haunt Jeannie.

Silva's former cabin, now in Jeannie's possession, had been meticulously searched from top to bottom, yielding no significant evidence. She had requested a local realtor inform her if the cabin ever went up for sale. When she received the notification, Jeannie seized the opportunity and purchased it as a retreat from her demanding role as the Assistant Special Agent in Charge at the San Francisco Federal Bureau of Investigation.

As Jeannie gazed through the window, the snowfall intensified.

Approaching the vibrant age of 45, Jeannie remained an attention-grabber whenever she walked into a room. Recognizing the escalating state of the real estate market, she believed her investment in the property could only appreciate, serving as a valuable addition to her retirement funds. And indeed, it proved to be true. Perched above the picturesque Coeur d'Alene Lake and surrounded by majestic Ponderosa pines and red and white fir trees, her abode resembled a perfect setting for a heartwarming Christmas movie destined for the Hallmark channel.

She had bought the property for another purpose as well - to conduct a thorough search of the grounds for any overlooked evidence by the forensic team in the hopes of finding closure. Unfortunately, her efforts so far had proved futile.

Following the acquisition of the spacious 3,000-square-foot, two-story log cabin, Jeannie made a startling discovery: her supposed mother was actually her aunt and her true biological mother was a wealthy widow who had resided in Myrtle Beach, South Carolina. However, her biological mother had already passed away. Unbeknownst even to her trusted confidant and right-hand man, Ismail Flores, Jeannie had become an incredibly wealthy individual, inheriting the entirety of her mother's vast fortune.

Now, it was time to put the cabin on the market before another real estate bust happened and property prices returned to a sensible level. She had made the trip to the cabin after she and her team finished up the case of terrorist bombings of several rollercoasters in various amusement parks in the United States. The actual bombers were now deceased, but the mastermind escaped, probably now safely back in Iraq. The case really drained her and, thus, the need to reset at the cabin.

She held a second hot cup of herbal tea as she pondered the rest of her life, both as an FBI agent and multi-millionaire. She loved her job, but the politics she had always attempted to avoid seemed to be spreading in the bureau and not just confined to D.C. She loved the bureau, but there was too much verifiable evidence showing major corruption in top management seeping into the various field offices and sub-branches.

Fortunately for her, her boss, SAC (Special Agent in Charge) Lomax, a forty-year veteran of the bureau, helped keep Jeannie under the radar, politically speaking. She had been in the spotlight a lot in the past several years while handling major investigations that brought recognition to her investigation skills.

Ismail Flores, her confidant and second in command, helped her solve a series of bombings in which jihads attacked attendees outside the Russian Orthodox Church in San Francisco while a second team attempted to do the same to people attending a presidential rally at the Cow Palace in Daly City. Initially, her team felt they had successfully resolved the investigation until they learned of a third team of jihadists who were planning to detonate a bomb over the underwater BART system tunnel between San Francisco and Oakland. This was avoided with the help of the Navy SEALs, and the terrorists were killed. Of course, the case was never reported to the public to avoid panic.

She realized that just reminiscing about these investigations seemed to raise her pulse, so she tried to turn her thoughts back to the snow. She saw a black Crown Vic enter her driveway and instantly knew it was a detective unit, probably from the Idaho State Police. Déjà vu, she thought. This was how she had been recruited as a consultant while on vacation. Well, actually, she was serving a suspension, and her ex-boyfriend, Sean Delaney, was working a case concerning an international group of hackers attacking first the Super Bowl broadcast and then national security.

She watched as Sergeant Max Elders got out of the driver's seat while another plainclothes officer did the same on the passenger side. The second officer carried a briefcase. "This will be interesting," she told herself. She opened the front door to the cabin while they were still approaching. "Sergeant Elders, what brings you out in this weather?"

"Hello, Jeannie. This weather is nothing. You should have seen it a few weeks ago." They reached the porch and stomped their shoes on the doormat as Jeannie invited them in.

CHAPTER 3

"Another serial killer on the loose or a consultation on those college students being killed in Moscow?" Jeannie glanced at the newcomer and offered a brief smile.

"Thankfully, we're not involved in either of those," replied Elders. "Jeannie," Sergeant Elders indicated his companion, "This is my new partner, Sergeant Gordon. I told him about the case we worked on together and how your expertise assisted in identifying the perpetrator. Once again, I'm hoping to get your insight on a case we're currently working on."

Jeannie shook hands with Sergeant Gordon. "How about a cup of coffee or tea? I also have some bagels and cream cheese if you're interested."

"That sounds great. Can I put my briefcase on the table?" Sergeant Gordon asked.

"Of course. Let me clear some space," Jeannie replied, gathering up the real estate documents she had spread out. "Please, have a seat. Is the situation in Moscow as dire as the media portrays? I've been hearing that the Moscow Police Department is overwhelmed."

"No, they actually have it under control, and there were some valuable forensic materials left behind that should assist in identifying the suspect or suspects," Sergeant Elders explained. "They're just trying to keep the media at bay while they make progress with the investigation. It was a harrowing scene for the first responders who arrived.

"The Moscow Police Department has already reached out to the BAU (Behavioral Analysis Unit) at Quantico for assistance in profiling the perpetrator. I suggested to my chief that we reach out to you as well, but I'm on his shit list for going over his head and contacting you without his approval. Even though we successfully solved that case involving the active serial killer who was abducting victims and hunting them down in a remote wilderness area, his ego is still a bit bruised."

"Wow, I'd be really interested to hear more about this Moscow case. It sounds intriguing, almost reminiscent of Ted Bundy's methods," Jeannie remarked. "However, I assume you didn't come all the way out here just to discuss that case. So, what brings you both?"

She arranged the bagels, cream cheese, and knives on the table before returning with two cups of coffee, along with Cremora and Truvia. "Apologies, there's no sugar available. Only these substitutes."

"That's all my wife and I use at home," Sergeant Gordon chimed in. "Although our current case can certainly wait, I must admit I haven't stopped boasting about how your insights played a pivotal role in identifying the serial killer we were dealing with. If you have the time, I would greatly appreciate hearing your thoughts on the Moscow college student murders," Elders requested.

"I've got plenty of time; I'm snowbound!" Jeannie replied with a laugh. "How much do you know about the case that hasn't been disclosed? I've been genuinely intrigued by it. Let's put aside any personal theories for now and focus on what the official investigation has concluded thus far," Jeannie suggested.

Sergeants Elders and Gordon took turns sharing the information they had been privy to. Jeannie attentively listened while refilling their coffee cups.

"So, what are your thoughts?" Sergeant Elders inquired while Sergeant Gordon started spreading cream cheese on a second bagel.

Jeannie took a sip of her tea before responding. "It seems like the work of a lone predator, possibly someone lacking adequate social skills and who experienced social awkwardness during their upbringing. They might even have been a target of bullying. The individual exhibits high intelligence and seems determined to showcase it to the world. They appear to be an outcast in most social settings, except when immersed in an educational environment. It's possible they could be a professor or a student. There's a notable presence of hostility in their actions."

Jeannie took another sip of her tea, contemplating her response. "As I mentioned earlier, I do see some similarities in this individual's personality to that of Ted Bundy. This perpetrator likely stalked their victims before the attacks and meticulously planned each step. They probably believe they won't get caught, and even if they do, they have the confidence and ability to talk their way out of it. I would venture to say that the motive behind these attacks is purely revenge, with no intention of theft or sexual assault.

"Based on what I've observed of the murder house from the news coverage, it's a strangely designed residence. It's entirely possible that the perpetrator, and likely the killer, could have accessed the second and third floors without ever entering the first level of the structure. However, considering the house has been described as a party house with frequent visitors, it's highly probable that the suspect had been inside before and was familiar with the layout," Jeannie explained.

Sergeant Elders glanced at Gordon, acknowledging Jeannie's insight. "I told you she was good. Now, what are your thoughts on the suspect? What kind of person do you believe is responsible for these murders?"

Jeannie took a moment to collect her thoughts before responding. "I believe the perpetrator is a white male, aged 25 to 35. Typically, these types of killers tend to target victims within their own race. He's likely single. You know, it frustrates me when well-meaning law enforcement officers mention catching the perpetrator to bring closure to the victims' families. The truth is, there is never true closure for the loved ones left behind. They will always be haunted by the questions of what their loved ones went through in their final moments and what their last thoughts were. It's something you never truly get over. It's a lifelong sentence for them."

"How about motive?" Gordon asked, hanging on every word Jeannie spoke.

"I haven't had the chance to read the autopsy reports, but based on what the coroner mentioned, it seems the victims weren't simply stabbed, but rather, they were violently torn apart. This leads me to believe that one or several of them were subjected to a disproportionate amount of rage from the perpetrator. My speculation is that the autopsy report will reveal that one or more victims, most likely the females, sustained most of the wounds," Jeannie concluded.

Sergeant Elders leaned forward, his gaze fixed on Jeannie. "Do you think there's a possibility of more than one person being involved in these crimes?"

Jeannie pondered for a moment before responding. "While it's possible for there to be an accomplice, such as a lookout or a getaway driver, I find it highly doubtful in this case. My educated guess is that the perpetrator might have made unwelcome advances toward one or more of the female victims, and they rejected him. This could have fueled his rage, which eventually exploded on the day of the attack. It appears to have been a planned event. I wouldn't be surprised if the investigation reveals that he had been surveilling the victims for days prior to the murders."

A solemn silence fell over the room as the weight of the situation sank in.

"I'll be sure to keep you updated on the progress," Sergeant Elders replied, politely declining another cup of coffee.

"So, what case are the two of you currently working on?" Jeannie inquired.

Sergeant Elders opened his briefcase and retrieved several photographs of the snow angel. The two investigators took turns briefing Jeannie about the details of the crime scene and the recently concluded autopsy report.

"We are operating under the assumption that the victim, Jane Doe at this time, was abducted and subjected to sexual assault until the perpetrator grew tired of her, eventually discarding her in the snowbank," Sergeant Elders explained. "Based on the rope and restraint marks on the body, she was tied up during the assault. Due to the depth of her body within the snowpack, we suspect she was likely thrown from the cab of a semi-trailer truck, which would explain the absence of tracks leading to the scene."

Jeannie studied the photographs intently, her focus unwavering. After a few minutes, she handed them back to Sergeant Elders. "You have an incredibly astute coroner. The way she determined the height from which the body was thrown before landing in the snowpack was truly brilliant. The calculations support her findings.

"As for my insights, I can't provide much more now. My instinct tells me that you should be searching for a trucker, and I believe this is not his first killing. The methodical and clean nature of the crime suggests he has been active for quite some time. If you manage to recover some semen and trace evidence, that could potentially be the key to eventually apprehending him."

Fortunately, we found semen but no other transfer evidence."

"No pubic hair?" Jeannie asked.

"None found. Perhaps he is just lucky, or he shaves himself," Elders replied.

"I apologize, but this case may turn into a 'who-done-it,'" Jeannie admitted with frustration evident in her voice, "and that really bothers me. If this were a bureau case and I were the investigator, here's how I would proceed," Jeannie continued. She picked up the photos once again, studying them intently before placing them back on the table. She finished her tea and got up to fetch some hot water.

"First and foremost, I would immediately gather all available security footage from truck stops, gas stations, fast-food restaurants, motels, and rest areas frequented by truckers. It's possible that by combing through those recordings, you might get lucky and find footage of the victim with her kidnapper. It's a time-consuming task, but it's crucial and must be done.

"Furthermore, I would recommend conducting a thorough search for missing person records of females, including runaways, who match the description of your victim," Jeannie advised. "If you come across a potential match, you can then proceed to investigate whether she had a cellphone and conduct a comprehensive examination of her phone records, including when it was last used, and analyze the cell tower pings.

"It's essential to reach out to her friends, boyfriends, employers, relatives, and neighbors to gather any relevant information. Did she mention anything about where she might be going? What was her mental state like? Was she considered a runaway? Damn, I don't envy you two.

"The bureau has tons of manpower that could be utilized to handle a lot of this legwork. I hope the Idaho State Police will pursue some of the things I have outlined. The guy has done this before, so run a check on similar body dumps. You might be able to triangulate his routes that way."

"What about motive? Can you give us anything to work with?" Elders asked.

Jeannie sweetened her new cup of tea with honey and settled back into her seat at the table. "Based on the information you've provided, I believe your suspect is a white male between the ages of 25 and 35, similar to the suspect in the college student murders. Considering the attractiveness of your victim, even in death, it's likely the suspect is somewhat handsome and physically fit, as these traits may have contributed to his ability to attract her. So, instead of searching for a bald, overweight trucker, focus on someone who fits this profile," Jeannie smiled, and the two officers chuckled in response.

As the conversation came to an end, the officers declined more coffee and expressed gratitude for Jeannie's insights into their case. They assured her they would keep her informed of any new developments. Jeannie watched them as they backed out of her driveway and drove away. She took the coffee cups and food items to the kitchen and placed the cups in the dishwasher. The remaining bagels and cream cheese were stored in the refrigerator. With these tasks completed, Jeannie made her way upstairs, her mind still occupied by thoughts of the college massacre. She decided to indulge in a long, hot bath, hoping to find some solace from the troubling cases.

CHAPTER 4

Jeannie awoke the following morning, beating the phone alarm she had set. Glancing out the window, she was pleased to see a clear sky and snow-free roads. "It's time to hit the road, girl," she said aloud. She packed her suitcase into the compact trunk of her car and decided to embark on a few hours of driving before finding a spot to have breakfast. With no pressing work obligations until the following Tuesday, she intended to relish the leisurely journey back to the City by the Bay.

Just after 8:15 a.m., Jeannie's cell phone rang, displaying Ismail's name on the caller ID. A smile lit up her face as she recognized his name. The two of them had endured countless trials together, and their unwavering support for each other had been crucial in overcoming the obstacles they faced. They had formed a bond that transcended mere colleagues and had become true allies.

"Hello, Ace. Did you miss me?" she asked playfully before he could even say hello. "I hope you've enjoyed my office because I'm on my way back, and you better start clearing out your stuff."

"Your office? It hasn't been yours for quite a while now. I've made a few improvements, though. I've added a hot tub, an 84" big-screen television, and a small refrigerator. The only thing left is to put my name on the office door," he replied with a mischievous tone.

"Did I tell you? The SAC (Special Agent in Charge) has arranged for your transfer to Nome, Alaska," she said, her voice filled with excitement. "I hope you like the dark since, on average, they only get five hours of daylight each day. But hey, as you never fail to remind me, you're a highly trained FBI agent, right?" she teased, her tone light-hearted.

"Alright, alright, I'll put your office back for you," he conceded, chuckling. "So, you're on your way back to God's country?"

"God's country? Well, I guess that depends on your perspective," Jeannie chuckled. "But yes, I'm leaving the great outdoors and returning to the concrete jungle of San Francisco. I'll see you bright and early on Tuesday. Is there anything pressing I should know about?"

Ismail replied, "No major emergencies. The SFPD may have a potential serial case, but I'll fill you in on all the details when you get here. Safe travels, boss." With that, he hung up the phone.

Ismail and Jeannie were like family to each other, and Ismail's family had become an extension of Jeannie's own. Ismail had been an agent for three years before Jeannie joined the bureau, and their paths crossed during their training. After spending some time teaching at the Behavior Analysis Unit in Quantico, Jeannie decided to request a transfer to the San Francisco area. It was the place of her birth and where her parents had lived before their passing. She longed to be close to her roots and her childhood memories.

Jeannie's life took an unexpected turn a few years ago when she received a call from an estate-planning attorney in Myrtle Beach, South Carolina, about the death of her biological mother.

During that challenging time, Jeannie made the conscious decision not to disclose to Ismail or her supervisor the remarkable revelation that her biological mother was a wealthy millionaire and that her inheritance had now passed on to Jeannie. It was a secret she chose to keep close to her heart as she grappled with the complexities of clearing her name from false accusations.

With the weight of her newfound wealth, Jeannie felt an added responsibility to navigate her personal and professional life with caution. The sudden wealth brought opportunities and potential pitfalls, and she needed to tread carefully to protect herself and those she cared about.

As she embarked on her journey back to San Francisco, thoughts of her inheritance mingled with the challenges she had faced. The knowledge of her substantial wealth added an extra layer of complexity to her already tumultuous life. Yet, Jeannie remained determined to forge her own path, relying on her skills and resilience and the support of her trusted allies.

With each passing mile, Jeannie contemplated how her newfound status would influence her future and how she could use it to make a positive impact in the world. The road ahead held uncertainties and possibilities, and she was ready to embrace them with a mix of cautious optimism and unwavering determination.

After a rather uneventful journey, she finally reached her home, skillfully coordinating her pit stops at fast food joints with much-needed bathrooms. It was the early hours of the morning, so she felt relieved, knowing that her vigilant yet nosy neighbor, Delores, wouldn't be lurking around. Both she and her husband were like watchful eagles, constantly surveying the neighborhood.

What made it slightly unnerving was the fact that they both possessed concealed carry permits and were always armed to the teeth. They treated Jeannie as if she were their daughter, often asserting their protective authority over her. Despite not having children of their own, their pride in Jeannie's esteemed position as a high-ranking FBI agent was unmistakable.

In Jeannie's frequent absences, the couple faithfully assumed the responsibility of looking after her residence. They took care of various chores, including putting out and retrieving her garbage can and ensuring her koi were fed daily. These beautiful fish thrived both inside her home aquarium and in the newly constructed backyard Japanese oasis, which featured an enchanting inground koi pond accompanied by a soothing waterfall.

Jeannie was taken aback by a delightful surprise when she visited her biological mother's opulent mansion in Myrtle Beach. To her amazement, she discovered a grand Victorian-style greenhouse perched on the edge of the Grand Strand overlooking the vast Atlantic Ocean. Within the confines of this magnificent structure, her mother had created a massive koi pond, exuding a sense of timeless elegance.

CHAPTER 5

Jeannie slumbered deeply, the sound of the doorbell merging seamlessly into her dream. As consciousness gently nudged her awake, she recognized the persistent chime as meaning someone was standing at her front door. With a hunch that it could only be Delores, she hastily snatched her robe, unconcerned about her disheveled hair, and descended the stairs. Pausing to peer through the peephole, Jeannie's eyes met the sight of Delores, also clad in a robe and adorned with oversized curlers that punctuated her hair like a quirky crown.

"Good morning, Delores. You're certainly an early bird. How's Walter doing?" "Oh, hi Jeannie. I'm glad you made it back home. All your fish are doing well. How was your trip to Idaho? Did you encounter any snow? Walter mentioned that Corvettes and snow don't mix well. By the way, we took care of your garbage can. You know, I had to send some stern letters to a few neighbors who neglected to follow our HOA rules. They need to ensure their garbage cans are out of sight by 5 p.m. on garbage day." Jeannie cherished Delores and her husband, but she sometimes wished Delores would take a pause and not chatter incessantly.

After what felt like an eternity, Jeannie managed to politely bid farewell to Delores. Finally alone, she prepared herself a simple breakfast and indulged in some much-needed relaxation. With a cup of coffee in hand, she found herself engrossed in the latest news, eagerly searching for any updates on the college student murders in Moscow, Idaho. Oh, how she longed to be involved in that investigation, to contribute her expertise and help bring justice to those affected. The thought fueled her desire, and she couldn't help but yearn for the opportunity to be called in on such a case.

At 10 a.m., Ismail gave her a call to ensure she had arrived safely at home. However, his tone was more playful whining than genuine concern, as he complained about being at work while she lounged at home in her jammies and bathrobe.

"How is SFPD doing on their serial?" she asked. "Any forensics to work with?" Jeannie inquired.

"Nah, no shell casings, so it appears the perpetrator used a revolver. That's why they suspect it's the work of a seasoned criminal. They'll follow the usual protocol, examining registered .22 owners."

"Good luck with that. Smart murderers don't use registered guns, and nearly everyone has a .22," Jeannie remarked, her attention divided between the conversation and the news report playing on Newsmax.

"How's the rest of the team?" Jeannie inquired.

"Oh, everyone is just peachy. They seem to appreciate my laid-back management style compared to your iron-fist approach," Ismail replied, bursting into laughter even before he finished his sentence.

"You're already on a roll today, aren't you, buddy?" Jeannie remarked with a playful tone. "But don't get too comfortable. Your taskmaster will be back tomorrow, so consider this an early warning."

As noon approached, Jeannie decided to step outside and pay a visit to the grocery store. Her cupboards were practically empty, prompting her to act. Opting for a hot roast beef sandwich from Subway, she carried it home to enjoy beside her serene koi pond. Just as she was enjoying her submarine sandwich, her cell phone rang, displaying an Idaho prefix. Without a doubt, she assumed it would be Sergeant Elders before she answered the call.

"Max, I mean, Sergeant Elders, how's it going?" Jeannie greeted him. "Please, Jeannie, call me Max. I almost feel like we're partners," he chuckled. "Are you busy? I can call you later if you'd like." "No, I was just about to enjoy a leisurely lunch. I head back to the bureau tomorrow. So, how's the investigation progressing?"

"You were right. We're dealing with a serial killer. Upon further investigation, we discovered more cases of missing females who matched a similar description as our victim. Their bodies were found dumped along the sides of various highways. Montana has five cases, and Washington also has five. We're still awaiting information from California and Oregon," Max shared.

"That's eleven victims across three states so far," Jeannie exclaimed, her excitement building as she realized the gravity of the situation. The possibility of the case gaining the attention of the FBI filled her with anticipation, yet she hesitated to bring up her eagerness to be involved. She decided to wait for the right moment to broach the subject, wanting to demonstrate her dedication and expertise when the opportunity presented itself. "Any luck on identifying your victim?"

"No, we are having photos taken of her face, and we hired a forensic mortician to doll the body up and look more human. We will start circulating it at the different truck stops and send them to those agencies that tentatively feel their victims might be part of this asshole's rampage."

"Sounds like you are on the right track, but as I said to you and your partner, there is a lot of work to be done," Jeannie replied.

"I have two reasons for contacting you," he explained, a sense of purpose underlying his words. "First, I wanted to provide you with this update. Second, I wanted to gauge your reaction to the possibility of us requesting your assistance, along with the bureau's, in apprehending this asshole."

There it was, the moment she had been eagerly anticipating. Jeannie knew that involving an agent from a different jurisdiction than the Idaho Bureau of the FBI was a possibility since there had been numerous cases in the past where a specific agent had been requested for assistance. However, the process would involve several steps. First, it would need the approval of Sergeant Elder's chief, which could be challenging considering their previous investigation had involved bypassing him. Then, the Idaho bureau would need to give their consent. Nevertheless, Jeannie felt confident that her Special Agent in Charge (SAC) would give the green light for the endeavor.

"What about your chief?" Jeannie questioned, fully aware of their strained relationship. She chuckled, adding, "I'm sure I'm also still on his shit list, pardon my French. As for the Idaho FBI, I have faith that my SAC could navigate that."

His tone turned more optimistic as he continued, "I've already begun working on my chief. I've been buttering him up, highlighting the positive press our department would receive if we joined forces and successfully apprehended this serial offender.

Surprisingly, he seemed intrigued by the idea, especially since he's been at odds with our new city manager regarding the budget lately."

"Well, alright then," Jeannie replied, a sense of determination in her voice. "You take the lead in getting the ball rolling with your chief and approaching the Idaho bureau, and I'll inform my SAC that such a request may be on its way. While the wheels of bureaucracy begin to turn, make sure to keep me updated. That way, when I arrive, I can hit the ground running and be fully prepared."

Bright and early the next morning, Jeannie's anticipation for the day ahead pushed her to wake up before her alarm clock went off. Knowing the unpredictable nature of the Dumbarton Bridge and Bayshore freeway, notorious for traffic delays, she didn't want to take any chances. Hurrying through her morning routine, she took a quick shower, leaving her hair to air dry in the cool breeze from the bay.

As she prepared breakfast, her mind wandered back to the college massacre that had left a lasting impact on her. The memories lingered, a constant reminder of the importance of her work and the lives she aimed to protect. Though the snow angel case demanded her attention, the weight of the college tragedy never truly left her thoughts.

After sitting down to enjoy a simple yet satisfying breakfast of French toast and a steaming cup of coffee, Jeannie took a moment to tend to her koi. She fed the vibrant fish in the aquarium in her dining room, finding solace in their graceful movements. Stepping outside to her custom-made koi pond, she repeated the ritual, ensuring the tranquility of her outdoor companions.

Dressed in a sharp, dark blue business suit, Jeannie felt ready to face the challenges of the day. With her trusted P226 Sig Sauer securely holstered on her hip, she left her home, determined and focused. Each step she took carried her closer to the unfolding events of the Snow Angel case, but the echoes of past tragedies reminded her of the urgency to seek justice and prevent further harm.

CHAPTER 6

The moment Jeannie stepped inside the bustling San Francisco bureau of the FBI, she was greeted by the familiar faces of Burk and Darcy, her two brilliant IT specialists. Their exceptional skills and expertise had played pivotal roles in the successful resolution of numerous high-profile cases. Despite the age difference, Jeannie felt a strong bond with them, akin to that of an older sister looking out for her younger siblings. It was a connection she cherished.

Burk, with his unruly mop of dark hair and an insatiable curiosity for technology, always seemed to have an answer to any digital conundrum. On the other hand, Darcy possessed a keen analytical mind and an uncanny ability to navigate the intricate depths of cybercrime. Together, they formed an invaluable team that complemented Jeannie's investigative instincts and field experience.

As Jeannie approached them, their eyes lit up with recognition and genuine warmth. Burk's face broke into a mischievous grin, and Darcy flashed a quick but warm smile. The trio exchanged greetings, instantly falling into their natural rhythm, their camaraderie evident in the way they seamlessly communicated and shared insights. The worst-kept secret was the fact that Burk and Darcy were actually a couple.

Jeannie had often relied on their technical prowess to decipher encrypted messages, track elusive online footprints, and unveil hidden digital trails. Their collective efforts had, time and again, propelled investigations forward, bringing justice to the victims and closing in on perpetrators.

Guided by mutual trust and respect, Jeannie, Burk, and Darcy formed a formidable team, blending their unique skills and perspectives to tackle even the most complex cases. Their shared dedication to their work and unwavering commitment to the pursuit of truth made them a force to be reckoned with within the FBI.

As Jeannie prepared to dive into the Snow Angel case, she couldn't help but feel a surge of gratitude for having Burk and Darcy by her side. Together, they were ready to unravel the mysteries, navigate the digital landscapes, and bring the elusive killer to justice. The bond they shared was not just one of colleagues but of a tightly knit family united in their unwavering pursuit of justice and determination to protect the innocent.

Jeannie made her way to her office and was greeted by her new secretary, Debbie. With her long-time receptionist on maternity leave, Debbie had taken on the role seamlessly, efficiently managing the day-to-day tasks and providing essential support. However, knowing her long-time secretary was out due to her pregnancy stirred bittersweet memories within Jeannie, reminding her of her own painful past.

Years ago, during her time at the Roseville field office, Jeannie and her partner Ismail found themselves caught in a harrowing shootout with urban terrorists. Tragically, during that chaotic event, Jeannie was shot and suffered a devastating loss—the life of her unborn son. The circumstances surrounding the pregnancy were clouded by the blackouts she experienced during her struggle with alcohol, a battle she had fought relentlessly to overcome.

The identity of the child's father remained unknown, a haunting mystery that Jeannie carried within her. Despite the pain and uncertainty, when she discovered she was pregnant, Jeannie had made a deeply personal choice. Firmly believing in the sanctity of life, she had decided to keep the child, even without knowing the paternal lineage. It was a testament to her pro-life stance and her unwavering commitment to the potential of every human life.

She had made a promise to herself never to let alcohol control her life again, and she had kept that promise, embarking on a journey of recovery and resilience. With a heavy yet determined heart, Jeannie acknowledged the complexity of her past and the scars it had left behind.

Taking a deep breath, Jeannie pushed the memories aside, reminding herself of the task at hand—the Snow Angel case, assuming the request from Idaho went through. "It's about time you come back and earn your keep," a smiling Ismail Flores said, carrying Jeannie a cup of coffee just the way she liked it.

"Ah, you missed me," Jeannie replied, her face beaming. "Is that cup for me?" she asked, already reaching out to take it.

"Yeah, now you're back, I have to get used to the old ball and chain. So, how was the trip? Did you solve any more serial cases for the Idaho State Police?" Ismail quipped.

"Funny you should ask. I had a visit from two of their finest, who are actively working on a serial case they call the Snow Angel. They will be requesting my assistance, so I was just joking about clearing your stuff out of my office. If Lomax (SAC) approves it, I'll be heading back to Idaho."

"That might take a while. I don't mind moving some of my stuff. As I've said before, a man with my talent needs a bigger office anyway," Ismail responded.

"Really?" Lomax interjected, entering Jeannie's office where they had just settled. "If you're considering moving up, we have that position we discussed in Nome, Alaska. It's still open, and I can process the paperwork right away if you're interested." Lomax glanced at Jeannie, trying but failing to suppress a smile.

"Oh, that's okay, boss. I was just joking. My little office is fine. I'll catch you later," Ismail swiftly exited the office while Lomax and Jeannie shared a laugh.

"I didn't mean to pry, but I overheard about the request for your assistance I'll be receiving from the Idaho State Police. Seems like your fame has reached the great northern part of the U.S. What's going on there?" Lomax inquired.

"While I was up there getting my cabin ready for sale, I ran into Sergeant Elders, the officer I collaborated with on that serial case where the suspect kidnapped his young victims and then took them into the wilderness of Idaho, hunting them down," Jeannie explained.

"Yeah, I remember. The guy thought the police were closing in on him, so he ended up killing himself after leaving a confession. It's pretty remarkable how that whole case came to a successful conclusion," Lomax remarked. Jeannie's heart raced, wondering if Lomax knew she had played a role in coaxing the perpetrator into taking his own life. Sometimes, the ends justified the means, or so she believed.

"A trucker discovered a young girl who had been thrown from the cab of an 18-wheeler onto a snowbank, hence the nickname 'Snow Angel.'

Sergeant Elders and his partner have been assigned to the investigation, and they stopped by to gather my insights on the case. Just before I returned home, they discovered there are eleven victims across several different states," Jeannie explained.

"Well, that certainly escalates it to a bureau case. I assume Sergeant Elders is initiating the necessary steps to formally request your assistance. Personally, I have no issue approving it, but you know how sluggish the Washington bureaucracy can be. Inform Flores that he can hold onto your small office since you're uncertain about when you'll be leaving us," Lomax instructed.

At 5 a.m., Officer Alisha Johnson of the SFPD struggled to keep her eyes open as she patrolled the vicinity of Golden Gate Park. Working nights while attending day courses at San Francisco State University was taking its toll, and testifying in court the previous day made it even more challenging to stay alert on the streets with only four hours of sleep.

She drove to her usual "stretch area," a small turnout where she could park her patrol car and take a walk in the hopes of rejuvenating herself in the cold San Francisco air. However, something caught her attention. It appeared to be a foot protruding from a cluster of large bushes. Curiosity compelled her to investigate further.

Approaching cautiously so as not to disturb a potential crime scene, she drew nearer. The grim reality sank in as she realized the truth. With each step, the fixed stare in the man's lifeless eyes and the gunshot wounds in his chest confirmed that she had stumbled upon a dead body. The number '3' written on his forehead in red left no doubt. She wasted no time and immediately called it in, alerting the authorities to the scene.

CHAPTER 7

"Hey, I just got off the line with SFPD homicide. Lieutenant Carlson informed me they discovered the possible third victim this morning near the entrance to Golden Gate Park. Their higher-ups are contemplating reaching out to us and bringing us on board. Just wanted to give you a heads up," Ismail shared with Jeannie as they arrived at the breakroom simultaneously.

"It's funny how things have changed," Jeannie replied with a sigh. "Back in the day, serial murder cases were rare. Now, it feels like we're dealing with them almost every week."

"Yeah, I remember those days back at the BAU," Jeannie reminisced, a touch of nostalgia in her voice. The main case studies we used in our lectures were

'The Manson Family,' 'Son of Sam,' and the 'Green River Murders' ... they were the main serials we focused on. It's surreal how today, we're dealing with these cases right in our own backyard. It's like that moment in Hitchcock's movie *The Birds* when the drunk in the Tides Bar looks up from his glass and says, 'It's the end of the world.' Everything feels so different now."

"Have you heard anything from Idaho yet?" Ismail inquired.

"No, it's still too early. Do you have any urgent tasks on your plate? I thought I would treat you, Burk, and Darcy to lunch," Jeannie responded.

"Oh, I'm ready, willing, and available. What's the special occasion? Are you taking the job up in Nome?" Ismail asked, a hint of humorous sarcasm in his voice.

"You wish," Jeannie chuckled. "No, I've been away for a while up north, and what better way to catch up on what everyone is working on than a working lunch? Of course, you don't have to come if you don't want to." She knew very well that when it came to offering Ismail food, it was a rhetorical question.

The four of them hopped into two bureau cars and made their way to a corner Chinese restaurant that Ismail had been raving about. Ismail took the wheel with Jeannie beside him as they decided to swing by the homicide department at the SFPD to gather any preliminary information, knowing that the investigation would likely fall into their hands.

As they settled into the restaurant and placed their orders, Jeannie turned to Burk and Darcy, asking, "So, what have you two been working on?"

Burk let out a sigh. "More never-ending paper chases," he replied. "This Bitcoin frenzy is attracting a lot of people who want to get rich quick, but instead, they end up losing their life savings. It's become quite a mess to untangle."

"Unfortunately, you're right," Jeannie nodded sympathetically. "These scams have become increasingly sophisticated, and it's often difficult to track down the perpetrators who operate from various international locations."

"It's a never-ending game of cat and mouse. I remember when it used to revolve around the Cayman Islands. So, what have you been up to lately?" Jeannie took a moment to gather her thoughts.

"Well, I've been up north taking care of some personal matters, putting my cabin up for sale since I'm rarely there," she replied. "But I've also been approached by the Idaho State Police regarding a serial murder case they're working on. We're still waiting for official confirmation, but it looks like I might be heading there soon to assist. It's been a bit quiet on my end lately, so I'm ready to jump back into the action. If things stay slow down here, I'll definitely be relying on you two to assist," Jeannie affirmed. "Unless, of course, you'd rather continue with the paper chase."

Burk and Darcy exchanged a quick glance before Darcy eagerly spoke up, "Count us both in!" she exclaimed with enthusiasm. Burk nodded in agreement, showing his readiness to switch gears and join Jeannie on the upcoming investigation.

Jeannie smiled, grateful for their commitment. "Great to have you both on board. Let's stay prepared for whatever comes our way."

"Agents Loomis and Flores here to see Lieutenant Carlson if he's available," Ismail informed the receptionist. They didn't have an appointment, but the receptionist called Lieutenant Carlson and granted them access. "Do you know the way?" she asked.

Ismail gave her a thumbs-up, indicating that they knew their way around, and they made their way to the homicide division. Ismail spotted Lieutenant Carlson first and walked up to shake his hand. "Well, what brings two of the FBI's finest to my humble abode? Hi, Jeannie, how are you doing? Is this old fart still giving you a hard time?" Carlson greeted them, shaking Jeannie's hand.

"That he is," Jeannie replied with a wry smile.

"Who's an old fart?" Ismail playfully responded, a smile on his face. "Seems like every time I turn around, I have to cover for her."

Jeannie rolled her eyes playfully, then turned her attention back to the matter at hand. "Heard you have a serial on your hands," she said, getting straight to the point.

"Not for long," Carlson replied confidently. "The Captain has already initiated the process to hand it over to you guys. Sorry about that. This one seems like a pro —.22 caliber, no shell casings, no forensics at all, and he's playing some twisted game."

Ismail and Jeannie exchanged concerned glances as Lieutenant Carlson revealed the disturbing pattern of the killer marking their victims with numbers. The gravity of the situation became evident.

"What kind of game?" Ismail interjected before Jeannie could. "Not for publication," Carlson replied, his tone serious, "But he's keeping track of his kills." Carlson walked over to one of his detectives' desks and retrieved a large envelope containing crime scene photos. He pulled out the photos, revealing the latest victim with the number '3' printed on his forehead.

"This is Sergeant Thompson, the lead on this case. He can't wait to hand it off to you."

Sergeant Thompson extended his hand, acknowledging Agents Flores and Loomis. Carlson introduced the two. "Nice to meet you both. You have quite the reputation with the recent major cases you've solved. I hope you have the same luck in tracking down this guy."

As the conversation continued, Sergeant Thompson provided additional details about the killer's modus operandi. "He used a red permanent marker on all three victims. The coroner believes he is right-handed. We don't have any casings or forensic evidence suggesting he either polishes his brass or uses a revolver. This guy is sharp."

Jeannie listened attentively, her mind already processing the information. "Do we have any potential witnesses or leads we can pursue?" she asked, eager to make progress.

Thompson shook his head. "We're working on it, but so far, no obvious connections or leads. It's as if the killer is deliberately keeping things random to throw us off. We've been stretched thin with the defunding issues, so your assistance is greatly appreciated."

Jeannie nodded understandingly. "We'll hit the ground running, Sergeant Thompson. Let's operate as if we've already been officially called in. We'll coordinate closely with your team, review the evidence, and work on uncovering any leads or patterns that may have been missed. By the time the paperwork catches up, we'll already be knee-deep in the case."

Carlson nodded in agreement. "That sounds like a plan, Jeannie. "If you could clear your morning calendar tomorrow, Thompson, it might save a lot of time if you brief Jeannie and her team regarding the cases and what avenues you have explored. What do you think?" Carlson asked, looking at Jeannie. "Just keep an eye on Flores there," he said with a playful smile. "He's not as young as he used to be."

Ismail laughed and retorted, "Who's old? I'll have you know that I'm still USDA prime!"

Jeannie chuckled and turned to Thompson. "Sorry about that. I haven't had a chance to send him to our shrink for evaluation, but you can see he still suffers from delusions of grandeur. Yeah, that sounds good if you are free, Sergeant Thompson. I'll send my IT team tomorrow to collect your reports and any available evidence, and we can start working together to catch this bastard before he strikes again."

"I love it when my boss talks dirty," Ismail said as the two moved to leave the homicide division.

"That sounds good. What time would you like me at the bureau?" Thompson asked.

"Does 11 a.m. work for you?"

"Sounds good. See you at eleven tomorrow."

As Flores and Jeannie left, Thompson turned to Lieutenant Carlson. "They do make quite the formidable team."

"I was not exaggerating when I said they are two of the FBI's finest. Their experience and skills are top-notch. If I were in the suspect's shoes and knew they were on my trail, I'd shit my pants. You better start boxing up all our reports and be prepared to turn it over to their team tomorrow."

Thompson nodded in agreement with Carlson's suggestion. "Will do. I assume you'll also be informing the Captain about the transfer of the cases to the FBI. I'm sure he can't wait to make a press announcement."

CHAPTER 8

"Number four should be an easy one, dude. She's like a stay-at-home mom or something. We can start spying on her tomorrow morning and see if she goes to work and, if she does, what she does about babysitting for her kids. I don't want her little ones left alone once we take her out. We even got a picture of her, so spotting her should be a piece of cake," a pleased Ariana said to her brother, Adam, who was drinking a Coke and eating potato chips on the couch.

"Well, number four, Jane Larson, is all yours, sis. Haven't heard much on the news about the first three targets. Obviously, the cops don't wanna admit there's a serial killer roaming around," Adam remarked, munching on another chip. "We just gotta be smart and make sure we leave zero evidence for them to trace back to us."

Jeannie gathered her entire team, giving them a heads-up to meet in the big briefing room at 10 a.m. Darcy and Burk had brought over all the case files, photos, and completion lists from the SFPD. Her plan, once Sergeant Thompson briefed her team, was to divide the investigation among her agents, assigning each of them a specific section. With any luck, they would get a clearer picture of the status of the cases and identify the areas that needed the most attention.

She was sitting in the break room when SAC Lomax walked in. "I haven't heard a peep from Jack Lasko, the SAC up in the Idaho bureau, regarding a request for you, but I know how bureaucracy can be slow as molasses," he commented. "So, what's the latest with you and your team? I noticed Darcy and Burk hauling in a load of boxes this morning."

"I was actually planning to swing by this morning but got swamped with a bunch of phone calls I had to return. Wanted to give you the heads-up that the SFPD has handed over their serial case to us. Three victims down and no leads. Seems like we're dealing with a pro here—.22 caliber, no shell casings, zero forensics. They're still going through the paperwork for the formal request, but I decided to take charge now in the hopes of nabbing the suspect before they strike again. Their lead investigator is coming over here at 11 a.m. to brief me and my team. Care to join?"

"I think I will take a pass on your briefing. Just keep me in the loop. So, you think it's a guy? Is 'he' the right pronoun to use in this messed-up world of ours?" he smiled.

"Who knows? It's gonna be a problem if D.C. starts trying to enforce that crap in this bureau. Ismail, for one, will go ballistic. Remember how he brushed off that diversity questionnaire?" Jeannie replied.

"Actually, I wish I had used some of his answers on that bullshit questionnaire. I think more people in our society need to stand up to those assholes pushing this woke shit, and maybe they'll back down. But hey, I'm getting old and can see retirement on the horizon."

"You can't retire, boss. You're like the rock that holds this San Francisco bureau together. We're in one of the most liberal cities, in a massive blue state, and yet you've managed to keep most of that crap out of here so we can actually do our job."

"Well, when I finally decide to hang up my cuffs, you can take over and keep up the crusade," Lomax remarked, sipping his coffee as he departed.

"It looks like she drops her kids off at the neighbor's house on the right. See her?" Adam handed the binoculars to his sister.

"Yeah, I see her. Start the car, and let's find out where she works. Maybe we'll get lucky and find a good spot for the hit. Tomorrow could be the day," his sister responded.

"A good day for us, but a bad day for her," Adam said, starting the car, ready to tail their target and discover her workplace.

"Alright, let's settle down. We have a lot to cover. I'm sure, by now, the rumor mill has shared the news that we are taking over the serial killer case for the SFPD. I want to introduce Sergeant Thompson, the lead investigator of the cases that are now ours." Jeannie turned on the laptop connected to the whiteboard showing pictures of the three victims. "Sergeant Thompson, this is my team," Jeannie said, stepping aside and joining Ismail by a side wall while the sergeant introduced himself.

Ismail leaned into Jeannie and whispered, "You know, that Sergeant Thompson is not a bad-looking dude."

"Will you behave," Jeannie replied, although she happened to agree.

Jeannie moved back over to the laptop. "Victim number one is Harold Patterson, African American, 56 years old," Jeannie began, addressing her team. "He's been married to the same woman for thirty years and has two grown children, a son and a daughter, both living out of state. His body was discovered in this alleyway behind the dumpster. As you can see, he was wearing a jogging outfit, and his wife confirmed that he had gone for his regular run. Unfortunately, he never returned home.

"Time of death was estimated between 6 and 7:15 a.m. The cause of death was two .22 caliber bullets to the heart, fired from close range. It seems our killer is keeping a tally of their kills. They marked a red number '1' on the victim's forehead using a permanent marker." Jeannie paused, allowing her team to process the information.

"Initially, we considered the possibility of a hate crime, given that the victim was black, but that line of investigation yielded no leads," Thompson explained. "The victim was still wearing an expensive watch purchased by his wife, suggesting that robbery was not a motive.

"Our coroner believes the two .22 shots to the heart were fired from approximately 1½ feet away, indicating the victim may have known the suspect, thus allowing them to get close. So far, we haven't checked the surveillance cameras in the area."

"Why not?" Burk inquired.

"Because of those damn liberals who rallied for defunding the police. They're now experiencing the consequences of their idiotic demands," Ismail interjected, frustration evident in his voice. "In other words, they're severely understaffed, and I mean severely."

"You are correct, Agent Flores," Sergeant Thompson replied.

Jeannie interrupted Thompson and addressed Darcy. "You know what? Darcy, could you come up here and start writing a to-do list on the other whiteboard? We need to put pressure on businesses with surveillance cameras to provide us with their footage. We also need to review any street cameras that might have captured something around the time of the murders. These action items will apply to all three cases. Sorry, Sergeant Thompson, please go ahead."

"Okay, let's move on to victim number two, Sheila Mayfield," he continued. "She was a 32-year-old divorced white female, a schoolteacher. She lived with her elderly mother. According to her mother, Ms. Mayfield went out to walk her dog. When she didn't return, her mother contacted a neighbor who happened to be a security guard. He went searching for Mayfield and found her behind some hedges. He noticed the bullet wounds and the fixed stare on her face, and based on his experience in Iraq, he knew she was dead. He called it in.

"The coroner determined that it was also a .22 caliber killing, with one shot to the heart and one to the head. Technicians discovered evidence at the scene suggesting that the killer dragged the victim behind the shrubs, leading us to believe it's a male suspect."

"It could be a strong female," Agent Marsha Gentry, known for her physical fitness, chimed in. Laughter filled the room, and a few other female agents clapped.

"Good point," Jeannie acknowledged.

Sergeant Thompson nodded before continuing. "Victim number three is Brad Haley. His body was discovered by one of our graveyard officers, who was out stretching her legs by a walking path near the entrance of Golden Gate Park. He was 67 years old, a retired stockbroker, divorced and remarried. He has three grown children who don't live at home. As you can see, a red marker indicated that this was kill number three."

"The preliminary findings from the coroner's examination indicate that the shooter stood approximately two to three feet away from the victim, mirroring the positioning in the previous two cases. The victim sustained two gunshot wounds to the heart, inflicted by a .22 caliber weapon. As of now, we're still awaiting the crucial surveillance camera footage. Jeannie, if you'd like, we can take a short break to use the restrooms and grab a coffee refill. During our next meeting, I'll assess the little progress we have made in the three cases and delve into the unexplored areas."

Agreeing with Sergeant Thompson's suggestion, the team took a brief respite to attend to personal needs and refresh themselves. Jeannie walked alongside Sergeant Thompson, heading toward the coffee table. A tinge of frustration colored his expression as he confided, "I can't help but feel foolish standing up there, updating your team on our current progress. It's disheartening to think about how much more ground we could have covered if we weren't so constrained by lack of funding."

He poured himself a cup of coffee. "I understand your frustration, Sergeant."

"Please, call me Jessie," he replied.

"Jessie it is. Sometimes, believe it or not, we have limited resources, like during the whole Covid thing, which hinders our efficiency, but we make the most of what we have."

Jessie sighed, accepting a cup of coffee. "We've been grappling with these shootings for weeks now, and it's starting to take a toll on everyone involved. Naturally, our Captain is relieved to hand them off to you and your team."

Jessie leaned against the table, sipping his coffee thoughtfully. "The information gleaned from the coroner's examination is significant, shedding light on the shooter's proximity and the caliber of the weapon used. The missing piece of the puzzle lies in obtaining that crucial surveillance footage."

Jeannie managed a faint smile, taking a sip from her coffee. "Well, let's use this break to regroup and strategize. When we reconvene, we'll discuss any potential leads and areas that may have eluded your attention. Fresh perspectives and collaborative thinking might illuminate new paths in the case."

Sergeant Thompson nodded affirmatively, sharing Jeannie's renewed determination. "Absolutely, Jeannie." With their determination rekindled, Jeannie and Jessie took the opportunity to gather their thoughts during the break. Ismail watched on, and Jeannie caught him with a smile on his face when he saw her with Sergeant Thompson. *My little buddy is right. He is very handsome.*

CHAPTER 9

Jeannie ran into Ismail as she returned to the briefing from the restroom, who, with his keen intuition, couldn't help but notice the subtle chemistry between Sergeant Thompson and Jeannie. As he observed their interactions and the way they exchanged glances, he couldn't help but sense a growing attraction between them. Being the perceptive and playful person he was, he found it amusing and heartwarming to witness the blossoming connection.

With a mischievous grin on his face, Ismail approached Jeannie, unable to contain his excitement. "Hey, boss lady! I think Sergeant Thompson likes you!" he whispered with a giggle, causing Jeannie to chuckle softly.

Blushing slightly, Jeannie playfully responded, "Oh, really? What makes you think so?"

Ismail nodded enthusiastically. "I see the way he looks at you and the way you smile when you're talking to him. It's like you two have a secret language only you understand."

Jeannie couldn't help but find Ismail's innocent observation endearing. She tousled his hair affectionately and whispered back, "Well, buddy, we're focused on the case right now, but who knows what the future holds? Let's see what unfolds."

As they regrouped with the team, Jeannie and Sergeant Thompson shared a knowing look, their connection silently acknowledged. While their primary focus remained on the investigation, a seed of possibility had been planted, and they both knew some things were best left to time and destiny. Out of the corner of her eye, Jeannie could see Ismail smiling.

Thompson concluded his briefing on the SFPD's efforts, handing over the investigation to Jeannie and her team. He characterized their work as a subpar police effort, influenced by the defunding policy endorsed by liberal city administrators, a decision that now haunted the city. His final words lingered in the room, underscoring the urgency of the situation: the intervals between the killer's strikes were diminishing, leaving no doubt that the relentless predator would continue until apprehended.

As Thompson meticulously detailed the SFPD's progress in the investigation, Jeannie's mind buzzed with a sense of purpose. With each point mentioned, she compiled an extensive action list, mentally assigning tasks to each member of her team. The mounting responsibilities reminded her that time was of the essence.

Deep down, Jeannie sensed the imminent call that would summon her for a temporary assignment alongside the Idaho State Police, delving into the haunting case of the snow angel killer. The chilling nature of the abductions and the macabre method of disposal weighed heavily on her thoughts, driving her determination to bring an end to the perpetrator's reign of terror.

Knowing her path would soon lead her away from the confines of San Francisco, Jeannie refocused her attention on the immediate tasks at hand. She would make every moment count, ensuring her team was well-prepared for the challenges ahead.

"Jeannie, that concludes our efforts for now," Sergeant Thompson stated, wrapping up their discussion. His words carried an undertone, hinting at unfinished business with sources they had reached out to but hadn't yet received a response from. "We've left our contact information, hoping that someone's security camera might have captured something of significance. If any leads emerge, I'll be sure to reach out to you."

As the conversation neared its end, Jeannie could sense a lingering curiosity in Sergeant Thompson's demeanor. An unspoken question hung in the air, and she patiently waited, allowing him the opportunity to address it on a more personal level.

Sergeant Thompson's words emerged hesitantly, his cheeks betraying a hint of blush as he broached the personal matter. "This may be a bit forward and presumptuous of me, but if you're unattached at the moment, I was wondering if you'd be interested in grabbing a drink together sometime."

Jeannie observed the slight change in his demeanor and recognized the courage it took for him to ask. She considered his proposition, appreciating the potential for a connection beyond their professional collaboration.

Jeannie responded with a warm smile, her interest evident in her voice. "If you're open to making it a dinner and allowing me to pay half, I would absolutely love that."

Thompson's smile widened, his traditional values shining through. "I don't know about you paying half. I'm old school," he replied playfully. "How about tomorrow night if you're available?"

"Tomorrow night works perfectly," Jeannie agreed, her excitement palpable. "If you have a place in mind, I can meet you there. This office can get pretty hectic, so it might be easier to coordinate that way."

Thompson nodded, considering the logistics. "Alright, let me think of a place, and I'll give you a call tomorrow morning. Looking forward to it." With those words, he made his way toward the exit, leaving Jeannie with a sense of anticipation for their upcoming evening.

Emerging from around the corner, Ismail approached with an unmistakable grin stretching across his face. Jeannie greeted him in a matter-of-fact tone. "Clearly, you overheard our conversation," she stated, not surprised by Ismail's presence.

Ismail's grin widened, a mischievous glimmer in his eyes. "Guilty as charged," he admitted, his playful demeanor evident. "But I couldn't resist witnessing the sparks flying between you two. I'm thrilled for you both!"

Jeannie's laughter blended with a deep sense of gratitude for Ismail's unwavering support and the lightheartedness he brought into her life. As they stood there, she was reminded that Ismail, who was much more than a mere co-worker, was her best friend.

Excitement surged within Jeannie as she contemplated the new chapter unfolding before her. Not only did she anticipate the challenges of the upcoming investigation, but she also yearned to share her newly formed intentions with Ismail and his wife. The inheritance from her mother's estate had bestowed a significant amount of wealth upon her, and she had made the heartfelt decision to assist them financially.

Knowing that Ismail's children would no longer need to worry about college tuition would alleviate a tremendous burden for their family. Jeannie regarded

Ismail's wife as a sister, and the thought of lightening their financial load brought her immense joy. She eagerly anticipated the moment she could reveal her plan and witness the relief and gratitude in their eyes.

Ariana and Adam sat in their car, their eyes fixed on their target as she parked near a bustling coffee shop and swiftly exited her vehicle. Ariana commented to her brother with a sense of familiarity and a hint of disdain in her voice, "She is so predictable."

As they watched, their target returned to her car a few minutes later, securing her drink before checking for traffic and resuming her commute to work. Adam, curious about his sister's plan, asked, "So, have you decided when you're going to do it?" His mind began to conjure up his own approach, imagining how he would carry it out.

Ariana's gaze remained fixed on their unsuspecting target. She grinned, a dark and twisted amusement coloring her words. "Right here. She gets so preoccupied with securing her coffee cup that she won't even realize someone is standing right next to her until it's too late. One shot to the head and one to the heart," she explained, relishing the details. Her voice dripped with a chilling enthusiasm. "The tricky part will be marking her as number four without anyone noticing. But hey, that's part of the thrill, isn't it?"

10

CHAPTER

Jeannie's night was plagued by restlessness, her mind consumed by vivid dreams of Jessie Thompson. With her extensive background in social psychology, complemented by her Ph.D. and years of experience studying serial killers during her tenure at the Behavioral Analysis Unit in Quantico, Jeannie possessed a depth of knowledge far surpassing that of the average homicide investigator. Many investigators may never encounter a serial killer case throughout their entire careers. Jeannie's unique expertise allowed her to navigate the intricate web of the killers' minds, providing valuable insights and a heightened understanding of their motivations.

As she awoke from her troubled slumber, Jeannie braced herself for the challenges that lay ahead.

The intertwining paths of her personal life and the relentless pursuit of justice converged, fueling her determination to unravel the intricate puzzle of the serial killer's psyche

revolving around the ongoing serial killer case. The looming knowledge of the next impending kill weighed heavily on her thoughts. However, interwoven with the darkness of the investigation was a glimmer of anticipation—her upcoming date with Jessie.

While taking a shower, her mind processed data like a computer. Much of the general public's knowledge concerning serial murder is a product of Hollywood productions. Story lines are created to heighten the audience's interest rather than to accurately portray the reality. By focusing on the atrocities inflicted on victims by "deranged" offenders, the public is captivated by the criminals and their crimes. This only lends more confusion to the true dynamics of serial murder.

Law enforcement professionals receive the same type of misinformation from a different source: the use of anecdotal information. Professionals involved in serial murder cases, including investigators, prosecutors, and pathologists, may have limited exposure to serial murder. Their experience may be based upon a single murder series, and they then extrapolate the factors in that case to other serial murders. As a result, certain stereotypes and misconceptions take root regarding the nature of serial murder and the characteristics of serial killers.

A growing trend that compounds the fallacies surrounding serial murder is the *talking heads* phenomenon. Major media outlets have their favorite 'expert' come on a show and showcase their know-how. Given credibility by the media, these self-proclaimed authorities profess to have expertise in serial murder. They appear frequently on television and in the print media and speculate on the motive for the murders and the possible characteristics of the offender without being privy to the facts of the investigation. Unfortunately, inappropriate comments may perpetuate misperceptions concerning serial murder and impair law enforcement's investigative efforts.

Jeannie recalled a lecture she gave at Quantico about the various myths around serial killers. Most serial killers are not reclusive, social misfits who live alone. They are not monsters and may not appear strange. Many serial killers hide in plain sight within their communities. Serial murderers often have families and homes, are gainfully employed, and appear to be normal members of the community. Because many serial murderers can blend in so effortlessly, they are oftentimes overlooked by law enforcement and the public.

She remembered using several killers to illustrate her point. Robert Yates killed seventeen prostitutes in the Spokane, Washington area during the 1990s. He was married with five children, lived in a middle-class neighborhood, and was a decorated U.S. Army National Guard helicopter pilot.

During the period of the murders, Yates routinely patronized prostitutes, and several of his victims knew each other. He buried one of his victims in his yard beneath his bedroom window. Yates was eventually arrested and pled guilty to thirteen of the murders.

The Green River Killer, Gary Ridgeway, confessed to killing forty-eight women over a twenty-year period in the Seattle, Washington area. He had been married three times and was still married at the time of his arrest. He was employed as a truck painter for thirty-two years. He attended church regularly, read the Bible at home and at work, and talked about religion with co-workers. Ridgeway also frequently picked up prostitutes and had sex with them throughout the period in which he was killing.

The BTK killer, Dennis Rader, killed ten victims in and around Wichita, Kansas. He sent sixteen written communications to the news media over a thirty-year period, taunting the police and the public. He was married with two children, was a Boy Scout leader, served honorably in the U.S. Air Force, was employed as a local government official, and was president of his church.

Jeannie also recalled talking about serial killers spanning all racial groups, contrary to popular belief. There are white, African American, Hispanic, and Asian serial killers. The racial diversification of serial killers generally mirrors that of the overall U.S. population.

Charles Ng, a native of Hong Kong, China, killed numerous victims in Northern California in concert with Robert Lake.

Derrick Todd Lee, an African American, killed at least six women in Baton Rouge, Louisiana.

Coral Eugene Watts, an African American, killed five victims in Michigan, fled the state to avoid detection, and murdered another twelve victims in Texas before being apprehended.

Rafael Resendez-Ramirez, a native of Mexico, murdered nine people in Kentucky, Texas, and Illinois before turning himself in.

Rory Conde, a Colombian native, was responsible for six prostitute homicides in the Miami, Florida area. Not forgetting female serial killers. They are perhaps the most cunning and forget about the myth that serial killers are only motivated by sex. There are many other motivations for serial murders, including anger, thrill, financial gain, and attention seeking.

Jeannie focused her attention on the serial case, trying to block out what lay ahead in the Snow Angel investigation. Most serial killers have very defined geographic areas of operation. They conduct their killings within comfort zones that are often defined by an anchor point (e.g., place of residence or employment or a relative's residence). Serial murderers will, at times, spiral their activities outside their comfort zone when their confidence has grown through experience or to avoid detection. Very few serial murderers travel interstate to kill.

To this point, the three numbered killings had all taken place within San Francisco's city limits. Jeannie checked the time on her watch and realized she had woken up earlier than usual. With time to kill and holding a steaming cup of coffee, she ascended the stairs to her home office, ready to dive into her investigative work.

Once inside her office, Jeannie positioned herself in front of the whiteboard, marker in hand. Methodically, she began to transcribe the known facts of the case onto the pristine surface. Each detail, each connection, and each lead were carefully documented, forming a visual representation of the investigation.

As Jeannie meticulously wrote on the whiteboard, her mind sifted through the information, searching for patterns, discrepancies, and potential breakthroughs. The whiteboard became a canvas of knowledge, serving as a focal point to organize her thoughts and guide her next steps in the relentless pursuit of justice.

Jeannie reached for her cell phone, snapping a quick photo of the items organized on the board. With a sense of urgency, she sent the image to Darcy, along with a request to transfer the contents onto the large whiteboard in the briefing room before the team's 9:30 briefing.

Aware of the importance of a well-prepared briefing, Jeannie wanted her team to have immediate access to the collected information. The whiteboard served as a visual aid, ensuring everyone could easily grasp the known facts, connections, and potential leads in the case.

Jeannie's message to Darcy emphasized the significance of having the information readily available. The upcoming briefing was a crucial opportunity for the team to discuss their findings and to strategize and collaborate effectively. With the image sent and the request made, Jeannie turned her attention back to the investigation, ready to delve deeper into the complexities of the case.

Why mark a number on their forehead? And no one has claimed responsibility to gain attention. I'm missing something.

CHAPTER 11

SAC Lomax waited patiently as Jeannie parked her Corvette in the bureau's secure garage. As she stepped out of the car, he greeted her with important news. "The official request for your assistance with the Idaho State Police came in late last night. You're cleared to go whenever you're ready. You might want to share the good news with your contact up there. How is your serial case progressing?"

Jeannie adjusted her bag on her shoulder, her determination evident. "We're just getting into high gear. The SFPD left several avenues for us to investigate. I have a briefing scheduled for 9:30 today. You're welcome to join if you're available."

SAC Lomax considered the invitation. "Maybe I will. Should I arrange refreshments, or has that already been taken care of?"

"Thank you, but I've already asked Darcy and Burk to handle it," Jeannie responded appreciatively. "Today, I plan to pass the reins of our investigation to Ismail. If everything goes well, I might leave for Idaho early tomorrow morning if that works for you."

A playful grin crossed Lomax's face as he considered the potential challenge. "Ismail might put up a fight, considering how small our office is, but we'll see. I'll see you at 9:30."

With their exchange concluded, Jeannie and Lomax prepared for the day's activities, their focus unwavering as they tackled both the ongoing serial case and the impending transition of responsibilities.

Making her way to the breakroom, Jeannie eagerly grabbed a cup of coffee to fuel her morning. With the warm beverage in hand, she headed to the briefing room to check on the progress. To her satisfaction, she found that Darcy had promptly displayed the information she had sent via text, ensuring its availability for the upcoming meeting.

Next on her list was a visit to Ismail's office, but she discovered that he hadn't arrived yet. Returning to her office, Jeannie decided to reach out to Sergeant Max Elders of the Idaho State Police. She dialed his number, and after just two rings, he picked up the call.

"Good morning, Jeannie," Sergeant Elders greeted her. "I found a note on my desk from our chief. Our request for your temporary assignment to our agency has been approved."

Jeannie couldn't help but feel a surge of relief and excitement.

"That's fantastic news," she exclaimed, now saying that she had learned of the approval from Lomax. "I'm leaving early tomorrow morning and should arrive at my cabin late tomorrow night if everything goes according to plan. I'll send you some random thoughts I have about our killer for you and your team to consider. Hopefully, I'll be able to visit your office in two days."

After ending her call with Sergeant Elders, Jeannie quickly composed a text message to share her thoughts with him:

> *"Most serial killers operate in distinct geographic comfort zones, often anchored to a specific location like their residence or workplace. They rarely travel interstate. However, the few who do typically fall into categories like itinerant individuals, homeless transients, or those whose professions involve extensive travel (e.g., truck drivers or military personnel). In our case, I believe our killer falls into the latter category. Their traveling lifestyle provides multiple comfort zones to operate within."*

As she sent the message, Ismail entered her office bearing two cups of coffee—one for Jeannie and one for himself. He couldn't resist teasing her. "Well, boss lady, how's the romance going with one of San Francisco's finest?"

Jeannie chuckled, appreciating Ismail's playful banter. "Wouldn't you like to know," she replied with a mischievous grin, her cheeks slightly flushing. "For your information, we're going out to dinner tonight."

Ismail couldn't contain his laughter, his amusement palpable. "Wow! Dinner, and then ... what? Drinks and hopes for something more?" Amused by his reaction, Jeannie shook her head playfully. "A girl doesn't kiss and tell," she retorted. "Besides, I'll be sharing all the details with your lovely wife; why would I divulge them to you?"

Jeannie gestured towards the empty chair, inviting Ismail to take a seat. She spoke in a serious tone, preparing to deliver important news. "Starting tomorrow, you'll be taking over for me. The request has been approved for me to assist the Idaho State Police in their Snow Angel murder investigation. I apologize for dropping a serial case on you, especially one with so many areas that still need to be thoroughly investigated. Unfortunately, the SFPD was severely understaffed and unable to give it the attention it deserved."

Ismail took a moment to process the weight of the responsibility being entrusted to him. He nodded, fully comprehending the gravity of the situation. "I appreciate your trust in me, boss," he began, a mischievous smile playing on his lips, "but like I said last time, I find your office a little too small for someone with my talent."

Just as Ismail anticipated Jeannie's response, SAC Lomax, who had overheard their conversation, entered the office at the opportune moment. He couldn't resist joining in the banter. "How about the janitor's closet? Would that fit you?" Lomax quipped with a hint of amusement in his voice.

Ismail, slightly taken aback, quickly recovered. "Oh, I was just joking, boss. I love working from Jeannie's office. You can count on me." He turned to Jeannie, his cheeks turning slightly red. "I'll see you at the briefing," he said before leaving.

The lighthearted exchange made Jeannie laugh. Lomax seized the moment to share an interesting tidbit. "Did you know that Ismail didn't put in for the Assistant Special Agent in Charge position in Fresno?" he asked, his tone curious. Before Jeannie could respond, Lomax continued, "I asked him why he didn't go for it. The guy is highly qualified. He told me that he's comfortable here, even though he dislikes the commute to and from the city. He didn't want to uproot his family and move to the raisin capital."

Jeannie chuckled, finding Ismail's dedication and commitment endearing. "He's a loyal one, that's for sure. We're lucky to have him on our team," she remarked, appreciating Ismail's choice to prioritize his family and maintain his presence in their current location. "I'm glad he didn't take the position. I know they would have selected him in a heartbeat but losing Ismail would be detrimental to the team. By stepping into my shoes when I'm called away, the team doesn't lose a step," Jeannie expressed with a sense of relief.

SAC Lomax nodded in agreement, a genuine admiration for Jeannie evident in his eyes. "Don't sell yourself short, young lady. I feel the same way about you being my second in command," he remarked, acknowledging Jeannie's skills and leadership. "Now, go charge up your team, and once you feel you can sneak out of here, go and beat the traffic. Needless to say, keep me abreast regarding that Snow Angel case up there."

With a nod of gratitude, Jeannie gathered her belongings and prepared to rally her team. She knew the importance of maintaining open communication with Lomax while she embarked on her temporary assignment.

CHAPTER 12

Eleven agents, along with Jeannie, Ismail, Burk, and Darcy, filled the main briefing room. The aroma of freshly brewed coffee and an array of breakfast treats filled the air. As everyone settled into their seats, SAC Lomax entered, completing the gathering.

"Alright, let's take a seat, please," Jeannie announced, capturing the attention of the room. The chatter subsided as everyone directed their focus towards her. "First and foremost, I want to inform you all that I will be leaving tomorrow for an assignment with the Idaho State Police. Agent Flores will step in as my temporary replacement, just as before. Now, you will see some of my initial thoughts on the board regarding the number murders. It's by no means comprehensive, but I believe it provides us with several avenues for our investigation. Ismail will assign your responsibilities."

Jeannie paused, allowing the team to review the action items displayed on the whiteboard. "I'd like to add the following to this initial list: The killer is due to strike again. As we all know, with a serial killer, the time between kills tends to diminish rapidly. While we currently operate under the assumption that the victims have been selected randomly, I hope that soon we can identify commonalities among them, which will greatly aid our investigation."

She glanced around the room, ensuring everyone was attentive. "I trust each and every one of you to carry out your assigned tasks diligently and to collaborate effectively. We have a challenging road ahead of us, but I believe in our abilities to bring this killer to justice. Let's get to work."

The room filled with a sense of determination as agents began discussing their roles and exchanging ideas. Jeannie knew she was leaving the case in capable hands and felt a renewed sense of purpose as she prepared for her assignment with the Idaho State Police.

Jeannie arrived home at 2:25 p.m., a mix of emotions swirling within her. She wanted to get in her house, pack for her early morning departure, and get dressed for her dinner engagement. She had arranged with Thompson to meet at a restaurant nearer to the Dumbarton Bridge on the peninsula so she could get home quickly after dinner.

She made her way next door to her neighbors' house, where Delores and Walter resided. They were known for being busybodies, so Jeannie felt confident her house would be well-watched during her absences. Though there were countless stories about her neighbors, Jeannie knew now wasn't the time to reminisce.

Before Jeannie could even ring the doorbell, Delores swung the door open. "Hi, Jeannie, is everything alright?" she asked, concern evident in her voice.

"Hi Delores, yes, everything is fine. But once again, I need to impose on you and Walter since I'll be leaving early tomorrow morning for an investigation," Jeannie explained.

Curiosity sparked in Delores' eyes as she leaned in. "Who are you going after this time? More modern-day Nazis, or perhaps the Communist Chinese? You know, I fear them more than those damn Russians. And don't even get me started on our own corrupt government."

Realizing Delores was getting carried away, Jeannie swiftly interjected, "It's just a murder case, Delores. They requested my expertise. I was wondering if you and Walter could kindly take care of my garbage and look after my koi—both inside my house and in the outdoor pond in my backyard?"

Delores's face lit up, seizing the opportunity to help. "Of course, Jeannie! Consider it done. We'll make sure everything is taken care of. Wishing you a safe trip."

Jeannie thanked Delores for her willingness to assist and bid her farewell. Relieved of that burden, she embarked on her journey back to her humble abode, filled with anticipation to perfect her appearance for the sizzling dinner rendezvous. Jessie had handpicked Ristorante Carpaccio, an exquisite Italian eatery nestled in Menlo Park, as the venue for their evening. Unfortunately, a mishap on the bridge caused Jeannie a ten-minute delay. Slightly flustered, she stepped into the restaurant with her heart aflutter and instantly spotted her date seated at the bar.

Adorned in an elegant black dress that perfectly complemented her matching shoes, Jeannie approached Jessie, who stood there in awe. "You look absolutely stunning," he exclaimed, casting an admiring glance over her. "Our table will be ready in fifteen minutes. How about a cocktail in the meantime?"

"I'd love a ginger ale, please," Jeannie replied. "I prefer not to have any alcohol tonight, as I want to ensure a good slumber. I have a long drive ahead of me tomorrow."

"Yeah, you said it was a request from the Idaho State Police," Jessie remarked, acknowledging the significance of Jeannie's involvement. "It must be quite a noteworthy case and an honor for you to be specifically called upon. Is it a classified investigation, or can you share some details?"

Jeannie paused for a moment, considering the question. "It's actually quite similar to the case we're currently working on," she explained. "They've dubbed them the Snow Angel murderer. The perpetrator appears to be enticing female victims while traversing various states' highways, only to abandon their lifeless bodies in the snowy banks along the roadways."

"Wow," Jessie exclaimed, his intrigue evident. "Do they have any leads on the Snow Angel murderer?"

Jeannie shook her head slightly. "Not that I'm aware of," she replied with a touch of concern. "The Idaho State Police are currently grappling with that brutal massacre of college students in Moscow. It's been quite a challenging time for them. Interestingly, I collaborated with their lead investigator in the past when we pursued a notorious serial killer. He would abduct his female victims and transport them by private plane to a remote region in northern Idaho, only to hunt them down for sport."

Jessie's recollection of the case brought back haunting memories for Jeannie. "The suspect eventually succumbed to his own guilt and took his own life. In his final act, he left behind a chilling note, revealing his victims' burial sites and even disclosing the location of the rifle he had used. It seemed like the mounting pressure of our investigation started to weigh heavily on him."

As Jeannie reminisced, she took another sip of her drink, the taste mingling with her memories of the clandestine operation she had orchestrated. She had infiltrated the suspect's residence and extracted a confession that exposed his heinous crimes. All because the liberal district attorney in that jurisdiction, despite the overwhelming evidence, had inexplicably refused to prosecute the suspect.

Jeannie's actions were fueled by a profound belief that the end justified the means. Driven by her relentless pursuit of justice and armed with an unwavering determination to safeguard society from a malevolent force, she had taken it upon herself to take what she saw as necessary measures. In her mind, the preservation of innocent lives outweighed any potential ethical or legal concerns.

It was a decision that carried great weight, laden with the moral complexities of vigilantism and the fine line between right and wrong. Jeannie knew her actions would be met with scrutiny, possibly even condemnation and arrest, but she firmly believed that the greater good was at stake. Sometimes, the established systems and authorities fell short, leaving a void that only individuals like Jeannie were willing to fill.

In her heart, Jeannie was driven by a profound sense of responsibility and an unshakeable determination to rid society of those who preyed upon the vulnerable. She held onto the belief that, in the face of darkness, her actions were a necessary means to achieve a more just and safer world.

Jessie's concern snapped Jeannie back to the present moment, and she offered a faint smile in response to his inquiry. "I'm sorry," she apologized, her voice tinged with a hint of melancholy, "I was lost in thought, reflecting on the numerous serial killer cases I've dealt with over the years. It's just that sometimes, I can't help but wonder about the countless predators who are still out there, inflicting harm on innocent people."

The weight of unsolved cases and the countless lives affected by these criminals weighed heavily on Jeannie's mind. Each unresolved case represented not only a tragedy but also the possibility that more lives were at risk. The thought of those unknown predators continuing their reigns of terror was a constant reminder of the work left to be done and the justice yet to be served.

Deep within her, Jeannie carried a relentless determination to seek out these criminals and ensure their terrible crimes came to an end. Her commitment to protecting the innocent was unwavering, and she was prepared to face the darkness head-on, one case at a time.

They received the long-awaited notification that their table was ready, and with courteous grace, Jessie guided Jeannie toward their designated spot. As he pulled out her chair, a gesture of chivalry, she couldn't help but appreciate his gentlemanly manners. The touch of his hand on her shoulder, though seemingly innocent, sent a subtle surge of electricity through her body, stirring a mixture of emotions, including a tingling hint of desire.

Jeannie ordered Melanzana Al Forno, which she read was eggplant baked with spinach and cheese in a pomodoro sauce. Jessie ordered Gamberoni Al Limone, which Jeannie learned was prawn sauteed with lemon, garlic, shallots, and cream served over risotto and green beans. "So, how long have you been with the bureau?" Jessie asked.

Jeannie smiled, appreciating the effort Jessie was making to start a conversation. She took a moment to think before responding. "Well, I've been with the bureau for about eighteen years now," Jeannie replied. "It's been quite a journey, but I find the work really fulfilling. How about you? How long have you been with the SFPD?"

I've been here for sixteen years. I'm sad at what the city has become and I'm thinking about transferring to a smaller city with less politics."

Jeannie really wanted to get to the elephant-in-the-room question and finally posed it. "Have you ever been married?" She watched to see how he would react to such a personal question.

Jessie looked a bit surprised by the direct question but appreciated Jeannie's honesty. He took a moment to gather his thoughts before responding, "No, I've never been married. I've been focused on my career for a long time, and it hasn't left much room for serious relationships. But I've always been open to the idea of finding the right person."

Jeannie nodded, understanding that their experiences in relationships might be different. She decided to be open about her own past. "I've been married twice," she admitted. "Both marriages ended in divorce. It's not something I'm proud of, but I believe in being honest. It took some time for me to learn from those experiences and grow as an individual. I'm hoping to find a meaningful and lasting connection now."

Jessie listened attentively, appreciating Jeannie's honesty and vulnerability. He realized they both had their own journeys and experiences, and it was important to approach their connection with an open mind.

"I think it's brave of you to be so open about your past," Jessie said sincerely. "We all have our stories, and what matters is the person we are now. I'm looking forward to getting to know you better."

Jeannie smiled, relieved by Jessie's understanding and acceptance. They continued their conversation, gradually building a deeper connection as they learned more about each other's lives.

They both skipped dessert but ordered coffee. Jeannie hoped it wasn't a mistake. She really hoped to fall asleep as soon as her head hit the pillow when she got home. It was obvious that they both wanted a second date as Jessie walked Jeannie to her car. "I didn't want to ask you at dinner, but how is the investigation going in its early stages?" he asked.

"Well, my partner, the one who was with me at your office yesterday, Ismail Flores, will take over my position while I'm up in Idaho. He and I worked out assignments, and all our agents are out beating the bushes. Hopefully, something will break soon."

"Wow! Is this your car? The bureau must pay well. What is it? A 2022 Corvette?"

Jeannie smiled as Jessie marveled at her car, appreciating his genuine reaction. She took a moment to respond, still feeling a mix of emotions about her inheritance.

"Yes, it's a 2022 Corvette," she confirmed. "But it's not from my FBI salary. After my parents passed away, I received an inheritance, and this was something I decided to treat myself with. It's been a fun ride, quite literally." She paused for a moment, contemplating whether to share more about her personal history. Finally, she decided to open up a little.

"You know, my biological mother also left me some money when she passed away. It was unexpected, and it's given me some financial freedom," Jeannie explained. "But for me, it's not about the car itself; it's more about the thrill and the freedom it represents."

Jessie nodded, listening attentively. He could sense that there was more to the story, but he didn't want to pry.

"Well, it's an impressive car, and I can understand why you love it," Jessie replied. "I'm glad you used your inheritance to treat yourself. It's important to find moments of happiness in life."

Jeannie appreciated Jessie's understanding and non-judgmental attitude. It seemed like they were both willing to accept and embrace each other's pasts, allowing their connection to grow.

As they stood by her car, they continued chatting for a few more minutes, enjoying each other's company. The anticipation of a second date lingered in the air, leaving them both eager to see where their connection would lead. Finally, Jessie leaned forward and gave Jeannie a quick kiss on the lips.

Jeannie felt a rush of warmth when he kissed her, and she couldn't help but smile. She appreciated his thoughtfulness and interest in staying connected while she was away. It was clear their connection was growing stronger.

"I would love to keep in touch, Jessie," Jeannie replied, her voice filled with genuine enthusiasm. "I'll make sure to update you on the case and let you know when I expect to be back. And I had a great time tonight, too." She reached into her purse and pulled out a pen, quickly scribbling her phone number on a piece of paper.

"Here's my number," Jeannie said, handing it to him. "Feel free to call or text me anytime. I look forward to hearing from you." Jessie took the paper with a smile and pocketed it carefully.

"I will definitely be in touch," he said, his eyes meeting Jeannies'. "Have a safe trip, and I'll eagerly await your updates."

They exchanged one more warm smile before Jeannie finally got into her car. As she started the engine, she looked at Jessie once more through the window.

"Take care, Jessie," she said, giving him a small wave. "Talk to you soon." With that, she drove off, feeling a mix of excitement and anticipation for what the future might hold for them.

CHAPTER 13

Ismail received the call from Lomax at 8:15 a.m. A body of a female had been found in front of a coffee shop near the financial district. Her forehead was marked with the number '4'. As soon as Ismail got off the phone, he kissed his wife and, without showering, drove to the scene. When he arrived, he saw the coroner and his team hard at work.

"Flores, where's your boss? Sleeping in, I suppose." Joe Montano, an overweight balding man with a drooping mustache badly in need of a trim, said with a smile as soon as he saw Ismail approach.

"No, she's been called away on another case. What do we have?" Ismail asked while trying to get a better look inside the vehicle containing the victim.

"Well, from her driver's license, her name is Jane Larson, mid-forties. As far as I can determine, she took one in the forehead and one in the heart. .22 caliber, I believe. Looks like the perpetrator was standing about here when he took the kill shots." Montano staged what he believed was the position the killer had taken.

"Thanks for the preliminary information, Joe. Anything else of note?" Ismail asked as he saw the bureau's forensic team arrive.

"No, that's about it for now. I will probably conduct the autopsy tomorrow morning if that works for you."

"That's fine. Just call my office and give me the time. Thanks, Doc."

Ismail turned to the forensic team leader. "Let's gather as much evidence as we can. We need to find any witnesses, review surveillance footage, and identify potential suspects. I want a thorough investigation. And don't forget to take photos of all the cars in the area. I know it's a pain, but it must be done. You won't be on your own. I called for all hands on deck."

As Ismail surveyed the area, his mind began to formulate a plan. He knew that the number '4' marked on the victim's forehead confirmed that the numbers killer had struck again. Jeannie was right; they were due to strike again. He instructed one of the forensic technicians to carefully photograph and document the marking on the forehead, ensuring it would be analyzed later.

"I want to know if there's any significance to that number," Ismail stated firmly. "It could be a personal message or a part of something larger. Let's not overlook any possibilities." He glanced at the victim's car, noticing the spilled coffee and the untouched holder where it had been placed. Ismail made a mental note to collect any potential fingerprints from the cup, hoping it could lead them to the perpetrator.

With a sense of urgency, Ismail began coordinating with his team, assigning tasks, and ensuring they followed proper protocols. He knew time was of the essence in solving this case and bringing justice to the victim.

As they worked, Ismail couldn't help but wonder about Jeannie and her whereabouts. He hoped she was safe and handling her own case well. However, he knew that for now, his focus had to be on the investigation in front of him, piecing together the puzzle and finding the answers they desperately sought.

Jeannie was making good time on her drive to Idaho. As she entered a fast-food restaurant, she was grateful for the chance to take a break from her long drive and clear her head. The familiar surroundings provided a sense of comfort, and she quickly placed her order before finding a seat by the window.

As she waited for her breakfast, Jeannie took a moment to reflect on the two different serial killer investigations she was currently involved in. While the thought of them being connected would have made her work easier, she understood that the reality was often more complex.

The Idaho case, she believed, involved a trucker using the interstates as hunting and disposal grounds and presented its own set of challenges. She hoped Sergeant Elders and his team of investigators were hard at work gathering evidence and collaborating with local law enforcement to narrow down the suspect pool. It was a painstaking process, but it had to be done to bring the perpetrator to justice and prevent further victims.

Conversely, the San Francisco Numbers case seemed to be an entirely different beast. The methods, victims, and patterns pointed to a distinct killer with a unique modus operandi. She felt that if they could come up with a motive for the killings, it would go a long way to identifying the killer. Ismail would find it, she was sure.

Jeannie's thoughts were interrupted as her breakfast was served. She thanked the server and began to eat, savoring each bite and allowing herself a moment of respite. It was crucial for her to recharge and nourish herself before diving back into the investigations.

As she ate, she couldn't help but let her mind wander back to her dinner date with Jessie. The pleasant memories brought a smile to her face, and she found herself looking forward to their next meeting. However, she reminded herself to stay focused on her work for now. Balancing personal and professional aspects of her life was always a delicate dance, and she wanted to ensure she gave her all to both.

After finishing her meal, Jeannie returned to her car, ready to continue her journey. Before she cleared the parking lot, her cell phone rang. Caller ID showed that it was Ismail.

"Good morning, Ace. You miss me already, huh?"

"Naturally, I miss you. Didn't Sherlock Holmes miss his Doctor Watson?" he replied. "I wanted to let you know the perpetrator struck again, victim number four. You were right. The kills are coming closer together timewise."

"Who was the victim?" Jeannie asked, stopping in the parking lot and turning off her car.

"A white female, forty-two years old, mother of two. She stopped at a coffee shop on her way to work, and the killer took her out when she returned to her vehicle. No shell casing and no forensics. We are canvassing the area, but with the killing committed down in the financial district, it's going to take time."

Jeannie's heart sank as she heard Ismail's update about the latest victim. The fact that the killings were becoming more frequent was alarming, and she knew they had to act swiftly to prevent further tragedies.

"Ismail, I know I don't have to tell you, but this is getting more urgent," Jeannie replied, her voice filled with concern. "We can't afford to let this killer continue to strike. We need to gather every available scrap of information. I think the key is the killer's motivation. Figure that out, and you should be able to connect the dots."

She paused for a moment, contemplating the situation and the potential connections between the victims. The timing and locations seemed too coincidental to ignore, yet there was a randomness to them.

Ismail sighed on the other end of the line, his voice reflecting the weight of the investigation. "We're doing our best, boss," he replied earnestly. "We're checking surveillance videos and actively following up on any and all tips and leads that come in. But as you know, these things take time. Lomax approved my all-hands-on-deck request. We won't rest until we find the person responsible."

Jeannie understood the challenges they faced, but her determination only grew stronger. She knew that time was of the essence, and they had to be relentless in their pursuit of justice.

"Ismail, please keep me updated on any developments," Jeannie said firmly. "I'll do everything I can to assist remotely. We need to collaborate closely. Two minds are better than one."

"Absolutely, boss," Ismail affirmed. "We'll stay in close contact, and I'll keep you informed. Stay safe up there."

As Jeannie ended the call, she took a deep breath, steeling herself for the challenging days ahead. The race against time had intensified, and she was determined to do whatever it took to bring an end to the killings and deliver justice to the victims and their families. With renewed focus, she started her car and merged back onto the road, her mind now filled with a heightened sense of urgency and determination.

As Adam sat on the couch sipping his beer and fixated on the television screen, a sense of satisfaction washed over him. The news report showed Ismail speaking to the coroner with the victim's body covered by a blue sheet. It was their latest kill, and the fact that the FBI had been called in meant their actions were garnering attention.

Ariana joined her brother on the couch, holding her own can of beer, and raised it in a toast. Their eyes met, filled with a sinister camaraderie as they celebrated their macabre achievements.

"Cheers to another successful hunt," Ariana said, her voice tinged with a chilling excitement. Adam clinked his beer can against Ariana's, a wicked smile spreading across his face.

"We're making headlines now, sis. The thrill of it all ... it's intoxicating."

They both took a sip of their beers, reveling in the moment. For them, the killings were more than just a means to an end; they were a twisted form of entertainment, fueling their dark desires and quenching their search for revenge.

As they continued watching the news coverage, they knew their spree had attracted the attention of law enforcement, and that only added to the excitement, the thrill of the chase. They relished the game of cat and mouse as they taunted the authorities with their carefully planned acts of violence.

The siblings were bound by a twisted bond, their actions intertwining their fates. They delighted in the chaos they created, savoring the fear and confusion they left in their wake while not losing track of their motivation for killing. For now, they both basked in the dark glory of their deeds, unaware of the imminent reckoning that awaited them.

CHAPTER 14

As Jeannie stepped out of her car and into the crisp Idaho air, a sense of tranquility washed over her. She was grateful for the safe journey and her cabin's familiarity; it was a place she could retreat to in the midst of her demanding work.

After opting to stop at a fast-food take-out place rather than have a sit-down meal, she entered her cabin with a Subway sandwich in hand, along with a bag of potato chips and a drink. As she stepped inside, she immediately felt a sense of warmth and coziness. The cabin held many memories and offered a respite from the challenges of her profession.

Setting her meal down on the kitchen counter, Jeannie noticed the real estate cards scattered across the surface. It seemed that people had shown some interest in her place, perhaps looking for a vacation getaway or a permanent residence in the area. The thought of potentially parting with the cabin tugged at her heartstrings, but she knew that her work often required her to be on the move. And now, with a mansion in Myrtle Beach, South Carolina, she didn't need the cabin.

She decided to open several windows to let the fresh mountain air in, allowing the cabin to breathe and invigorating her senses. The view outside was serene, with towering pine trees and a glimpse of a nearby lake. Despite the chilly weather, the beauty of the surroundings brought her a sense of peace.

Jeannie sat down at the kitchen table and enjoyed her meal. As the evening drew on, she decided to place a call with Sergeant Elders to let him know she had arrived and set up a time to meet at his office. He answered on the third ring.

"You made good time," he said before she could speak.

"Yes, with no snow to contend with, the only time I had to stop was for a restroom break. So, anything transpire while I was on the road?" Jeannie asked, hoping that there had not been any more snow angels reported.

"No, no new murders, and I have a list on a board in our training room showing our investigation to date. I can't wait for you to look at it. I'm sure we have missed a lot; we need your expertise."

"What time would you like me to show up tomorrow morning?" Jeannie asked.

"You probably want to sleep in. How about 10 a.m.?" he responded.

"As tired as I am, I doubt I will be able to sleep very well since I want to get a jump on the investigation. How about 8 a.m.?" Jeannie asked.

"That's great for us. I will call the other detectives and have them here at nine so you have time to look over what we have done so far. See you in the morning." With that, he hung up, and Jeannie headed to her bedroom.

As Jeannie approached the Idaho State Police Department in Coeur D'Alene the next morning, she couldn't help but admire the scenic view of the lake. The substation was situated in a prime location, surrounded by natural beauty. She parked her car in the designated area and made her way inside.

Entering the building, Jeannie was greeted by a bustling atmosphere. Officers were going about their duties, and the sound of radios filled the air. She headed toward the reception desk and introduced herself to the officer on duty.

"Good morning," Jeannie greeted him with a smile. "I'm FBI agent Jeannie Loomis, here to see Sergeant Elders."

"Oh, hello," the officer said as he stood and shook Jeannie's hand. "He is expecting you. Welcome on board. The meeting is taking place in the conference room on the second floor. You can take the stairs or elevator over there," he pointed in the direction.

"Thank you," Jeannie replied and followed the instructions, deciding to take the stairs to the second floor and get some exercise in. She found the conference room easily, thanks to the signs posted along the hallway.

As Jeannie entered the conference room, she was greeted by Sergeant Elders and an older man who turned out to be the substation Chief. She exchanged pleasantries with them before settling in to discuss matters with Sergeant Elders. However, before she could get comfortable, the Chief requested a private conversation in his office. Jeannie couldn't help but wonder if she was in for a scolding regarding her previous collaboration with Sergeant Elders on a serial case when they went above the Chief's authority.

Leaving her briefcase and notepad on the table, Jeannie gave a playful wink to Sergeant Elders and followed the Chief out of the room. She knew she would miss out on catching up with the information displayed on the whiteboard, but duty called.

In the Chief's office, he gestured for Jeannie to take a seat across from his desk. He began by expressing his gratitude for her assistance on the serial killer case. He mentioned the media's moniker for the investigation, the 'Snow Angel Killer,' and the pressure they were under to solve it promptly due to the attention it had garnered, even receiving calls from high-ranking officials.

Jeannie replied, "Thank you, Chief. I'm hopeful that your team of investigators and I can bring the killer to justice swiftly. Sergeant Elders impressed me during our previous collaboration, and I'm looking forward to working with him and the other members of your force."

The Chief then revealed that it wouldn't only be the Idaho State Police involved in the investigation. The chiefs and sheriffs from other states where bodies had been found had agreed to form a joint task force, and they collectively requested that Jeannie lead the unit. He let that information hang in the air, waiting for her reaction.

Jeannie smiled and responded, "Thank you for the vote of confidence. I'm honored to lead the task force and eager to work with them."

Then, the Chief's expression turned serious, and he confessed his initial frustration with Jeannie for going above him on a previous serial killer case. He questioned the seemingly neat resolution of the case, where the suspect had allegedly committed suicide, and left a note indicating the victims' burial sites. He suspected there was more to it than met the eye.

Jeannie maintained a composed demeanor, feigning genuine interest as the Chief continued to watch her closely. He revealed that the suspect owned the only donut shop in town and had a close relationship with the district attorney, who happened to be a frequent customer and benefitted from free coffee and donuts.

The Chief believed this friendship played a significant role in the district attorney's refusal to charge the suspect despite substantial evidence.

Pausing for a moment, Jeannie carefully considered the Chief's words. She understood that he didn't buy into the theory of the suspect's suicide. Meeting the Chief's gaze directly, she responded, "Having taught at the BAU in Quantico, specializing in the study of serial predators, I've learned that delving into the mind of a killer is challenging. We may never truly understand why he chose to take his own life. However, we can find solace in the fact that there is one less predator among us, and that's a positive outcome, isn't it?"

Jeannie's response left the Chief to ponder her words, and she maintained her calm and collected façade, concealing her actions that terminated the killer after extracting his confession. "Well, I better go meet my task force. I will keep you abreast of any progress we make," and with that, Jeannie got up and left the Chief's office.

Jeannie found her way back to the briefing room and heard a lot of noise coming from the interior. Sergeant Elders saw her and pointed to a table with coffee and pastries. "So, what did the Chief want?" he asked.

"Oh, you know, welcome on board, whatever you need, blah, blah, blah. So, let me get a cup, and you can tell me about what you have up there on the whiteboard." By the time Elders had completed his review of the material on the board, the room had filled with investigators. "Well, I guess we need to get started, huh?" Jeannie said.

CHAPTER 15

Jeannie took a moment to review the information that Sergeant Elders had displayed on the board. As she processed the details, she quickly jotted down some notes and thoughts, preparing herself to contribute to the discussion.

Once she felt ready, Jeannie glanced at Sergeant Elders, gave him a subtle nod, and indicated she was prepared for him to begin. With that signal, Sergeant Elders called for everyone's attention, prompting the detectives in the room to settle down and focus on the meeting.

"Okay, let's settle down," Sergeant Elders addressed the room. "For those of you who don't know me, I'm Max Elders from the Idaho State Police. I appreciate all of you being here on such short notice. Today, we have the privilege of having FBI Agent Jeannie Loomis with us. We specifically requested her from the San Francisco Bureau office. Agent Loomis was an invaluable asset in our previous serial killer case, where the perpetrator kidnapped women and hunted them in the wilderness. I'm sure many of you have heard about her and her team's involvement in several major investigations, including the jihadists who targeted several amusement parks across the U.S."

Sergeant Elders' mention of Jeannie's past accomplishments seemed to strike a chord with the detectives in the room. Conversations sparked among them as they recognized the significance of having someone with Jeannie's expertise and experience standing beside Sergeant Elders.

Jeannie stood confidently next to Sergeant Elders, observing the reactions and conversations taking place. She maintained a composed demeanor, ready to contribute her knowledge and skills to the case at hand. Jeannie knew that building trust and establishing effective teamwork would be crucial in solving the Snow Angel investigation, and she was prepared to work alongside the dedicated detectives in the room to bring the killer to justice.

It was now Jeannie's turn to introduce herself. "Thank you, Sergeant Elders, for your nice introduction. I remember the late Red Skeleton who, after receiving a warm welcome just for walking onto a stage, would turn to leave, thinking it was not going to get any better." Everyone in the room laughed.

“Ladies and gentlemen, and please don’t ask me to use pronouns,” Jeannie took a moment to bask in the laughter that followed her comment. It helped set a positive and lighthearted tone for the rest of her introduction. Once the room had settled down, she continued speaking,

“We have our work cut out for us. It is obvious by the number of kills that this is a very proficient predator who has been operating for a long time. What I’m saying is that we have quite a task ahead of us. It’s evident that the predator is highly skilled and dangerous. He is very comfortable with the method he uses to entice young women to enter his big rig, and with the highway systems he travels.

When Sergeant Elders and his partner first briefed me on this case, one conclusion became clear to me. This individual is not only using the Interstate Highway system as his hunting ground but also as a convenient way to dispose of his victims.” She paused for a moment, allowing her words to sink in before continuing.

“I strongly believe that by focusing our efforts on the highways, we can uncover critical clues that will lead us to him and, ultimately, bring him to justice. The interstate system offers both opportunities and challenges for a predator like him. It provides an easy means of moving between locations, but it also leaves behind a trail of evidence if we know where to look.” Jeannie made eye contact with the detectives in the room, emphasizing the importance of their role in the investigation.

"Our goal will be to meticulously examine the highways, searching for any signs of suspicious activity, unusual behavior, or evidence that may have been left behind. We'll work closely with local law enforcement along these routes, pooling our resources and sharing information to create a comprehensive strategy. As I said, there is a lot of work to be done. I'm confident that with our collective expertise and determination, we can bring this predator to justice and ensure the safety of our communities."

Jeannie's words conveyed her confidence in the team's abilities and her commitment to the task at hand. She believed in the power of collaboration and the strength that came from a united effort. The room filled with a renewed sense of purpose as the detectives prepared themselves to tackle the challenge together.

Jeannie took charge of the situation, recognizing the importance of getting the task force up to speed efficiently. She devised a plan to divide the attendees into teams representing their respective states. She quickly jotted down the states where the killer had dumped bodies and tore out pages from her notebook, distributing them strategically on tables throughout the room.

"Alright, everyone," Jeannie addressed the room, "it's time to break into teams. Each table represents a state where the bodies have been found. We have Washington, Idaho, California, Montana, and Oregon. Take a moment to find your state, grab some coffee, use the restroom, and when we reconvene, please sit at the designated tables with your corresponding place marker."

She encouraged the detectives to move around the room, ensuring they had a chance to gather refreshments and take care of personal needs before regrouping. Jeannie understood the importance of creating a conducive environment for focused discussions and teamwork.

As the room buzzed with activity, the detectives located their assigned tables and formed groups based on their respective states. They began to gather, ready to share their expertise and knowledge while strategizing for the investigation ahead.

Jeannie and Elders observed the detectives engaging and felt a sense of unity and purpose envelop the room. Each team would bring their unique insights and local knowledge, contributing to the collective effort of solving the Snow Angel case. She was confident that this collaborative approach would strengthen the task force and increase their chances of success.

Before restarting, Jeannie checked with Elders to see if arrangements had been made to have some food delivered so the task force could have a working lunch. "No, I didn't think about that. I thought everyone would just do their own thing since our budget is very tight right now."

"Don't worry; the bureau can cover it," Jeannie said. In reality, she was going to pay for the food. "While

I'm working with the task force, call around and find a restaurant that can deliver some sandwiches, potato chips, soft drinks, etc. Here is my credit card so you can pay for it, and I will put in for reimbursement when I get back to San Francisco. This looks like a hungry group, so order a lot. They can take home any leftover food."

"Alright. Everyone appears to have found their table. Now, here is your assignment for the rest of today.

"First, I have arranged for lunch to be brought in so we can continue our work during lunch. See Sergeant Elders if you have a specific dietary requirement. Your assignment for the rest of today is to review your own state's case files and compile a comprehensive report summarizing the key findings and any relevant evidence. Pay close attention to any discrepancies, missing information, or potential leads that need further investigation. I want you to provide a clear and concise analysis of the case, outlining the strengths and weaknesses of our current position.

Then, I need you to draft a list of follow-up actions and tasks that need to be completed in the coming days. This should include any interviews to be conducted, evidence to be gathered or analyzed, and potential collaboration with other departments or agencies. I want you to be brutal. I know it is tough to criticize other law enforcement officers, and no one likes constructive criticism, but it must be done.

Once you have completed the report and the list of follow-up actions, be prepared to present it to the task force tomorrow morning. We will reconvene tomorrow at 8 a.m. to discuss the findings and determine our next steps. Each team will report to the group, so pick a spokesperson or two." Everyone got busy laying out how their group wanted to tackle the task at hand. Sergeant Elders rejoined the meeting.

"Subway was the best bet. They will deliver the food at 11:45. I hope that is alright."

"Works for me; I'm already famished." She glanced at her watch. "Is there a vending machine? I think I need something to hold me over until lunch." Elders walked with Jeannie down the hall and pointed out the vending machine.

"Man, I have to say, I'm impressed. In just a few minutes, you got twenty-one investigators from different jurisdictions to roll up their sleeves and work together," a smiling Elders said as he waited for Jeannie to make her selection from the machine.

"Thanks, but that is the easy part. The tough part will be to process their information and come up with a plan of action. But I agree; the task force has come together in a short amount of time."

"Remember, this is a critical case, and we need to work efficiently and diligently to make progress. If you have any questions or need assistance, don't hesitate to reach out to me. Let's get to work and make sure we leave no stone unturned."

CHAPTER 16

Jeannie arrived back at her cabin clutching a stack of reports that provided her with a glimpse of what she anticipated the task force would delve into during their presentations the following morning. Along the way, she had made a quick stop to gather groceries, opting to prepare spaghetti using her cherished grandmother's secret sauce recipe. With a bottle of red wine in hand, she poured herself a glass and savored its taste as her cell phone interrupted the tranquility. Glancing at the caller ID, she saw it was Ismail.

"Have you already cracked the case, Ace?" she inquired casually, taking a sip of her wine.

"Almost there. Just need to tie up a few loose ends," Ismail responded before adopting a serious tone. "Actually, we now have four victims. Early this morning, a woman in her forties was discovered fatally shot right outside a coffee shop in the financial district. Unfortunately, there were no witnesses, but we're searching for any surveillance footage. She had the number '4' written on her forehead. How's your case progressing?"

"Well, before my arrival, the chiefs and sheriffs responsible for the body dump sites in the five states formed a unified task force called the 'Snow Angel Killer Task Force,'" Jeannie explained.

"Well, that's original. You're really building up your reputation; a regular rockstar, huh?" Ismail's remark carried a hint of admiration with a lot of humor attached. "So, legendary leader, have you managed to crack your case yet?"

"Not a chance, smartass," Jeannie replied, chuckling softly. "As I mentioned, the killer has been dumping bodies across five states that we're aware of, and who knows how many remain undiscovered. The only thing we know for sure is that the perpetrator seems to prefer blond victims and relies on the interstate freeway system for swift getaways.

Tomorrow, each member of the task force will provide updates on their respective state's cases, and hopefully, we can collaborate and brainstorm some new investigative avenues. But, just like yours, the time between kills is escalating, adding to the complexity of our investigation."

"What about you?" Jeannie inquired. "Lomax has given you carte blanche to hunt down this bastard."

"Yeah, I'm aware," Ismail replied. "I've assigned Burk and Darcy to comb through the social media profiles and cell phone records of the four victims, but it's a time-consuming process. I don't anticipate finding much in their bank records, but Stevenson and Murray are looking into that aspect as well. I have a hunch that if we can uncover a common thread among the victims, it'll propel us in the right direction. On another note, has lover boy reached out to you yet?" Ismail teased.

"If you're referring to Jessie Thompson, no, he hasn't," Jeannie replied. "He knew I'd be knee-deep in shit up here. But just so you know, we did have a pleasant dinner last night, and he was a complete gentleman throughout."

"What's the fun in that?" Ismail chuckled.

"How does your wife tolerate you?" Jeannie asked playfully.

"Hey, when she's married to a Portuguese stud muffin like me, I can do no wrong," Ismail quipped.

"While I'm up here, I'll see if I can find a good psychiatrist who can help with your grandiose ideas," Jeannie jokingly remarked. "I'll check in with you tomorrow. Stay safe."

"Same to you, boss lady," Ismail replied before ending the call.

As Ariana's brother, Adam, woke up from his nap, Ariana greeted him with a dark smile. "Well, four down and ten more to go," she whispered, her voice filled with a chilling excitement. Adam blinked, trying to shake off his drowsiness. "What are you talking about, Ariana?"

Ariana leaned closer, her eyes gleaming with a twisted enthusiasm. "I did some digging online while you were sleeping. Our friend at the crime scene this morning, FBI Agent Ismail Flores, is quite the decorated agent. Fifteen years of experience solving major cases alongside his supervisor, Agent Loomis."

Adam's eyebrows furrowed as he absorbed the information. "So, we've got their attention," he murmured, a mix of concern and intrigue in his voice. "They might not be expecting people like us, but we can't underestimate their skills."

Ariana nodded, her mind already whirling with plans. "Exactly, Adam. That's why we have to be more careful than ever. These agents have seen it all, and they won't go down without a fight. But imagine the thrill of outsmarting them, of staying one step ahead. It's a challenge we can't resist."

Adam's expression grew serious as the gravity of their situation sank in. "But we mustn't get careless," he cautioned. "We've been successful so far because we've been meticulous, covering our tracks and leaving no evidence behind. We can't afford to make a mistake now with ten more targets to hit."

Ariana's eyes sparkled with a dangerous intensity. "Don't worry, Adam. We won't slip up. We'll continue to be meticulous and calculated in our actions. And we'll make sure Agent Flores and Agent Loomis never see us coming. Who's next on the list?" she asked as she looked down at a sheet of paper showing four names crossed out with ten remaining.

As the siblings shared their dark resolve and reviewed their lists of targets, their twisted bond grew stronger. They were fully aware of the risks and the game they were playing with law enforcement. With their newfound knowledge about Agent Flores, they were determined to stay ahead. However, the cat-and-mouse game had taken a dangerous turn, one that would test their limits and push them to the edge.

At 2:15 p.m., Ismail returned from the scene of victim number four and, after a quick stop at the restroom, made his way to the larger briefing room. He had contacted Burk from the scene, requesting that he inform all team members not at the financial district crime scene to attend a briefing at 2 p.m. However, he found himself running fifteen minutes late.

"Good afternoon, everyone. Apologies for my tardiness. It's been a busy day so far," Ismail began as he entered the room. "For those who are not yet aware, we've taken over the serial murder investigation from the SFPD. This morning, we added victim number four to the list of murders.

The SFPD has admitted that their previous three homicide investigations didn't receive the thoroughness they would have in the past. Unfortunately, they are severely understaffed in their investigation division due to the defunding police nonsense."

He paused for a moment, surveying the room, and continued, "To expedite matters, I want you all to form teams of four and, essentially, reinvestigate the first three homicides. Burk, Annette, and I will focus on today's murder. Darcy, I want you to serve as the central point of contact where everyone can send their information so we can enter it into your 'magic' database."

Addressing the team directly, Ismail expressed his thoughts on the investigation. "Here's what I believe: If these killings aren't random, they're undoubtedly connected in a way that only the killer currently understands. Our goal is to uncover that connection between our victims, which will ultimately lead us to the suspect. I realize that everyone hates to bad mouth another investigator's work, but we have no choice. Find the holes in their investigations. What else should have been done? Create an action list. Be prepared to share your work with the group tomorrow. Let's reconvene here at 9 a.m. in the morning."

As the team members dispersed, their minds were filled with a mixture of determination, curiosity, and a renewed sense of purpose. They understood the importance of their work and the urgent need to solve these interconnected murders. With Ismail's guidance and the combined efforts of the team, they were determined to bring an end to this vicious cycle of violence and ensure justice for the victims.

CHAPTER 17

Jeannie endured a lengthy and draining day. When Sergeant Elders invited her to join his family for dinner at his house, she politely declined, expressing her desire for a refreshing hot shower and an early bedtime instead. Anticipating another demanding day ahead, she believed that once each group delivered their presentations, they would unite and devise a strategy to apprehend the individual causing trouble.

Jeannie discovered a KFC store and decided to grab a meal to go along with a diet Dr. Pepper. She couldn't help but acknowledge that old habits die hard. Placing her food in her cabin's microwave to keep it warm, she headed for the shower. The hot water worked wonders, relieving the stiffness in her shoulders and neck. As she was getting out of the shower, she heard her cell phone ringing. Assuming it was Ismail, she took a seat near her vanity, allowing her hair to fall naturally.

"Loomis," she answered, glancing at the caller ID displaying 'unknown.'

"Hi, Jeannie. It's Jessie. How's everything up there?" the voice on the other end greeted.

"Hey, Jessie. It's great to hear from you. As expected after our first day, progress in the case is still slow. Eleven murders so far, and unfortunately, it seems like another one is looming. How about you? How have things been going?" Jeannie replied.

"No complaints here. Solve one homicide, and two more pop up. And that's not even counting the daily overdose cases we're dealing with. The city offering free needles and safe injection zones isn't helping matters," Jessie lamented.

"Yeah, it's disheartening to witness what that once beautiful city has turned into. And if you venture into Oakland across the bridge, it's just as bad. Let's not even get started on the politicians who talk a big game but do nothing," Jeannie expressed with a hint of frustration.

"Has Agent Flores made any headway with our previous cases?" Jessie inquired.

"Not much, except that they picked up victim number four early this morning," Jeannie replied.

"I heard about that when I arrived at work. Honestly, I feel more confident with the bureau handling these cases. Still no leads?" Jessie asked.

"Not that I'm aware of. Flores had just left the crime scene when he called me. Seems like another random shooting—no forensics, no witnesses stepping forward with useful information," Jeannie explained, her voice tinged with disappointment.

"Oh, well, I wish him luck. I wanted to tell you again how much fun I had with you at dinner the other night. I'm also glad you didn't go Dutch on the bill. Like I said, I'm old school, and that is the macho thing to do," he said, trying not to laugh. "So, obviously, you have no idea when you will be returning to Wacko, California?"

"I'll pass on your good luck wishes to Flores. And thanks for mentioning it again, Jessie. I had a great time at dinner, too. Don't worry; I will never force you to go Dutch on a bill. I understand the old-school macho code," Jeannie replied playfully. She could sense his suppressed laughter.

"As for my return to 'Wacko, California,' I'm afraid I don't have a concrete answer yet. It all depends on how quickly we can make progress in this case. But rest assured, I'll keep you posted," Jeannie assured him.

James Rivas drove his tractor-trailer rig through Look Out Pass on Interstate 90, heading towards Mullan, Idaho to refuel. This stretch of the road was the point where Idaho welcomes a person from Montana, offering a spectacular view that had lost its appeal over time. The lookout showcases the picturesque valley surrounding Mullan, Idaho, but to truly appreciate it, one would have to divert their attention from the constant curves of the road ahead.

Upon reaching Love's Travel Stop, James Rivas stepped out of his cab and stretched his weary limbs. After refueling his truck, he maneuvered his rig to join the other parked tractor-trailers. Ensuring everything was securely locked, he made his way into the restaurant to satisfy his hunger and to potentially encounter any adventurous ladies seeking a ride.

The next morning, Jeannie had arranged for a catering service to provide breakfast at the Idaho State Police substation for her task force team members. She quickly grabbed some French toast, sausage links, and a much-needed cup of coffee before being joined by Max Elders.

"Jeannie, you're spoiling us," Max exclaimed, foregoing the usual greeting. "The bureau must have an incredible budget. Look at this plate. Pancakes, sausage, bacon, hash browns. It's like heaven."

"Be careful, Max. Indulging too much might send you to heaven sooner than expected," Jeannie responded as the Chief unexpectedly took a seat at their table, sipping his coffee. Both Jeannie and Max were caught off guard by his presence.

"Mind if I join you this morning? Max informed me about the agency reports on the victims," the Chief said casually.

"The more, the merrier," Jeannie replied with a forced smile.

"You've laid out quite a spread for the task force, and I noticed the car you're driving. The FBI must pay well," he remarked with a hint of sarcasm.

"Well, actually, the bureau is covering the breakfast expenses," Jeannie lied, well aware that it wasn't the truth. "And as for the car, let's just say it's a way of 'spending your inheritance,'" she added, not completely lying.

"Oh, I'm sorry to hear that. Your husband passed away?" the Chief inquired.

"No, my mother and father," Jeannie replied, opting for a partial truth. She could have mentioned her biological father, mother, and stepmother, but she saw no reason to divulge further details to the Chief.

Observing Max's nod and understanding the signal, Jeannie stood up. "Well, I suppose we should get started if you're ready, Max," she said. Without saying anything to the Chief, Jeannie walked up to the front table where her Mac laptop was set up. As the task force members noticed the activity, they began returning to their respective tables. Another officer brought in an additional whiteboard to accommodate the presentations. Jeannie checked her computer connections and confirmed that the large screen behind her was activated.

"Does any group want to volunteer to go first?" Sergeant Elders asked.

Lieutenant Taylor from the Shasta County Sheriff's Department in California raised his hand. Slightly overweight and sporting male pattern baldness, he stood and stated, "We're ready to present. Would it be possible to use your laptop up there? We've put together a PowerPoint which should make it easier for everyone to follow."

Jeannie welcomed him to the front and inserted his thumb drive into her Mac's USB port. She and Elders decided to yield the table to the California group and joined the other task force members, taking their seats.

Jeannie stole a quick glance at her notepad, where she had hastily scribbled the newly acquired details about the recent body discoveries reported to Sergeant Elders. The count had escalated to twenty-one victims as California and Oregon disclosed six and four bodies, respectively, in their states. Had she been aware of the killer's extensive spree beforehand, she would not have assigned the task force that they were now planning or reporting out.

California

1. Sophia Bennett – 16 years old, blond, Hawthorne, California
2. Emily Collins – 13 years old, blond, Los Angeles, California
3. Olivia Parker – 17 years old, blond, Fresno, California
4. Ava Mitchell – 22 years old, blond, Eureka, California

5. Isabella Hayes – 24 years old, blond, Lake Shasta City, California
6. Mia Anderson – 16 years old, blond, Redding, California

Oregon

7. Charlotte Thompson – 27 years old, blond, Medford, Oregon
8. Amelia Foster – 31 years old, blond, San Francisco, California
9. Harper Campbell – 41 years old, blond, Denver, Colorado
10. Scarlett Adams – 15 years old, blond, Fargo, North Dakota

Montana

11. Chloe Cooper – 33 years old, blond, Tulsa, Oklahoma
12. Zoe Ramirez – 37 years old, blond, Las Vegas, Nevada
13. Lily Morgan – 34 years old, blond, Memphis, Tennessee
14. Grace Sullivan – 15 years old, blond, Boseman, Montana
15. Stacey Peterson – 21 years old, blond, Pittsburg, Pennsylvania

Washington

16. Victoria Reed – 40 years old, blond, Miami Beach, Florida
17. Stella Phillips – 26 years old, blond, Memphis, Tennessee
18. Penelope Turner – 38 years old, blond, Charlotte, North Carolina
19. Nora Peterson – 14 years old, blond, Los Angeles, California
20. Aurora Ross – 15- years old, blond, Butte, Montana

Idaho

21. Ruby Mitchell – Idaho

"My God," she thought. "How could this guy have been operating this long without getting caught?"

Just before Taylor launched into his presentation, Jeannie's mind swiftly shifted gear, strategizing the perfect way to transition from their previous assignment to the new avenue she intended them to pursue. She recognized the importance of delivering a compelling speech that would captivate her team and inspire their dedication to the upcoming task. Jeannie knew she needed to craft her words with finesse, weaving a narrative that would ignite their curiosity and fuel their determination.

"Excuse me, Lieutenant Taylor. I need to address the team," Jeannie said, advancing toward the lead table. Taylor sat down in front of the computer, not sure where Jeannie was heading.

Jeannie looked at her entire team, taking a pause for effect. "Now, brace yourselves because I'm about to drop a bombshell that might make you temporarily hate me, but please don't because we're a team here." Several officers laughed while others had smiles on their faces, not sure where Jeannie was going.

"So, here's the deal: Forget the state-by-state reporting on victims and your investigations I asked you to prepare for today. Why? Well, it's time to put the pedal to the metal, folks! After I received the latest lists of victims from California and Oregon, that added ten more kills to the list, bringing a total of twenty-one victims. The time between kills is rapidly diminishing, leaving us with little breathing room between these heinous acts. In other words, we're in the fast lane now, my friends!"

Lieutenant Taylor slowly rose with two of his officers and walked back to the table representing California, realizing that, at least for now, he was off the hook having to make a presentation. After he took a seat, Jeannie continued.

"But fear not, for your hard work won't go unnoticed. Your previous efforts will be the catalyst for our grand investigative adventure! Think of it as an upgrade, like going from a trusty old Crown Vic to embracing the thrill of a sleek, powerful Corvette! Trust me, I wouldn't steer you wrong, pun intended." She could hear some of the officers inform others that the red Corvette outside that everyone had noticed upon their arrival was Jeannie's car.

CHAPTER 18

Jeannie turned her back on the task force members engaged in hushed conversations and confidently approached the whiteboard. With notepad in hand, she swiftly jotted down a series of numbers: 13-41 on the first row, 31-41 on the second, and 13-27 on the third. The room fell into a curious silence as Jeannie turned around, wearing a knowing smile, and addressed the group.

"Alright, folks, gather around, and let's dive into some intriguing detective work." Everyone began to laugh. "Thanks to Sergeant Elders' updated victim list from California and Oregon, I took the liberty of breaking down the ages of our unfortunate victims during breakfast. Pay close attention to this column here," Jeannie pointed to the first row on the whiteboard, "which represents the youngest to the oldest victims, ranging from thirteen to forty-one years old."

Leaning in, she continued, "Now, look at this second line, my friends. These victims fall within the age group of thirty-one to forty-one. Let's call this the older group for now. And finally, on the third line, we have the younger group, encompassing those victims aged thirteen to twenty-seven."

Jeannie's sharp gaze swept across the room, taking note of the engaged expressions but also recognizing that not everyone fully comprehended the significance of the age breakdown. With a thoughtful pause, she devised a method that would utilize this newfound information to assign tasks to the task force members, capitalizing on the killer's potential preferences.

"Now, my brilliant investigators, let's put this age breakdown to work in a way that guides our next steps," Jeannie began, her voice filled with conviction. "It's evident that the killer demonstrates a preference for younger victims within the 13-27 age range. We'll leverage this knowledge to assign specific tasks and delve deeper into our investigation."

She continued, outlining the plan. "I want each state to come up with a list of victims, organized by age and time of death. We'll scrutinize the data, focusing on the earliest and latest kills within each age group. By pinpointing when the first kill occurred and tracking the timeline up until the most recent one, we can establish a clearer understanding of the killer's progression and movements."

Jeannie's gaze swept across the room once more, her tone brimming with determination. "And here's the twist, my extraordinary team. We know the last kill took place in Idaho, so we'll work backward from there. By tracing the timeline and connecting the dots, we'll unravel the intricate threads where we might find the underlying motive for the killings and identify any patterns or targeting methods employed by our elusive killer."

With a renewed sense of purpose, the task force members set their sights on the assignment ahead, ready to uncover the truth hidden within the age breakdown and follow the trail that would lead them closer to apprehending the cunning killer.

"Okay, so each group will come up with a list based on age and time of death. Oh, and include the interstate where the bodies were found. More importantly, today will be a working lunch, so how does pizza sound?"

After settling the bill for his meal and pocketing the receipt, James Rivas made his way to the restroom. Exiting the facility, a sudden craving for a quick snack led him to the small grocery store adjacent to the truck stop. He casually strolled through the aisles, selecting a couple of candy bars and a soda to keep his energy up until his next overnight stop. Little did he know that his routine detour would reveal an unexpected opportunity.

And there she was—a woman with beautiful shoulder-length blond hair and an attractive figure. In that instant, something within James sparked. A chilling certainty took hold of his mind. She was the one, the next target in his sinister game. She was talking on the phone, so he got close enough to eavesdrop.

"No, I'm okay, really. I've made it to Idaho. If I can hitch a ride from a trucker heading into California or at least Oregon, I hope to make it to Hollywood by Wednesday or Thursday at the latest." She laughed, and Rivas found himself smiling. Now was the time for him to turn on his charm.

After a few minutes, the young female said goodbye and hung up the payphone. "Sorry, I didn't mean to overhear your conversation, but you did say you were heading to Hollywood, right? I can give you a lift. I'm going to San Francisco, which is a lot closer to LA than this place." He smiled, showing off his bleach-white teeth. It's the least I can do," Rivas said, his voice laced with an air of charm. She smiled and laughed, not believing her luck had changed so quickly.

"Yes, and it shouldn't be too hard to find a ride from San Francisco down to LA. I'd love a ride if you are sure it's okay?"

Rivas stepped closer, his eyes locking with hers. "Hollywood, that's quite a journey, but with a little luck and the right company, anything is possible. Consider me your lucky charm," he added, flashing a confident smile.

As they exchanged a few more words, Rivas's charm was at its peak. He knew the time had come to make his move, to lure her into his web of deception. With every calculated word and charismatic gesture, he played the role of the charming stranger, disguising the darkness that lurked beneath his affable facade.

"My name is Tiffany," she said as they walked to Rivas' rig.

"I'm James. Where you from?" he asked as he positioned himself behind the wheel.

"Believe it or not, but I'm from the state of David Crockett – Tennessee."

"Tennessee. Damn girl, you've come a long way. By the way, that's the first time I ever heard anyone call Davy Crockett David."

She smiled and giggled. "Most people aren't aware that David Crockett really didn't like being called Davey. It all started with an actor who went around the country acting like Crockett, and the first name was shortened to Davey."

"It's going to be a really interesting ride to California. Let's hit the road, girl."

19

CHAPTER

Ismail, following the precedent set by Jeannie, had bagels, cream cheese, and assorted pastries waiting for his team when they arrived. Lomax invited himself when he heard pastries were on offer. With a cup of coffee in hand, Ismail called the group to order. Lomax grabbed another pastry and left the briefing room.

With Darcy's help, the victims' pictures had been taped to the large whiteboard in the room. She had obtained their vital information from various sources and placed that information under each photo.

Victim #1. Harold Patterson – Fifty-six, African American male

#2. Sheila Mayfield – Thirty-two, white female

#3. Brad Haley – Sixty-seven, white male
#4. Jane Larson – Forty-three, white female

"Thanks to Darcy, we've got the photos of the four victims up here on the whiteboard arranged in the order they were tragically taken from us," Ismail Flores announced, acknowledging Darcy's contribution. A ripple of amusement passed through the room.

"Now, folks, let's not rush to hasty conclusions here," Ismail continued, a playful tone lacing his words. "If we look at the victims, we can see a diverse pattern emerging. Two victims are of white ethnicity, while the other two are individuals from minority backgrounds. But hey, let me remind you all that realization and a quarter won't even buy you a cup of coffee these days. I mean, seriously, where can you still find a cup of coffee for just a quarter? It's a sign of the times, my friends."

The room erupted in laughter, agents exchanging amused glances. One of them couldn't help but tease Ismail, commenting that he must have witnessed the era of inexpensive coffee firsthand. In response, Ismail theatrically raised his eyebrows, pretending to scrutinize the agents in attendance as if searching for the cheeky culprit who made the remark.

The lighthearted moment served as a brief interlude, fostering a sense of camaraderie and easing the tension in the room. Ismail appreciated the agents' ability to find humor amid the serious nature of their work, strengthening their connection as they collectively prepared to face the challenges that lay ahead.

Ismail took a few moments to study the photos as the room became silent. Then, with a determined expression, he turned to address the task force. "Alright, team, my gut tells me that these killings are far from random. There's a motive at play here, and if we want to crack this case swiftly, we need to uncover the connections between each victim," Ismail declared, his voice filled with conviction.

"Darcy, I'm relying on your exceptional skills. I want you to dive deep into every aspect of these victims' lives. Scrutinize their social media accounts, bank records, cell phone activity, and even their arrest records, if any. Leave no digital stone unturned. We're counting on you to unearth any potential leads or associations."

Turning his attention to the rest of the task force, Ismail continued, his words carrying a sense of urgency. "As for the rest of you, it's time to hit the ground running. I want you to go back and conduct thorough interviews with family members, neighbors, and anyone who may have crossed paths with these victims. Cast a wide net. We're looking for any sliver of information that can shed light on a possible connection between these four individuals. While you are out there, visit the crime scenes. Locate all surveillance cameras. Check with store owners. See if anyone in the area has a porch camera. We might luck out. If you get any static from anyone not wanting to give up pictures, contact me, and I will take care of a warrant request."

He paused, letting the weight of the task sink in before emphasizing the importance of collaboration. "Remember, every piece of information you gather must be forwarded to Darcy. She'll work her magic and create a comprehensive database that will guide us toward the killer. We're all in this together, and it's through our collective efforts that we'll bring this perpetrator to justice." Ismail's eyes scanned the room, his voice unwavering, "Remember, stay focused, stay determined. The killer last hit this morning. It appears the killings are only seven days apart, so we have six days before he strikes again."

Ismail helped himself to another cup of coffee and a bagel, which he smothered with cream cheese. Burk approached him. "What assignment do you have for me?" Ismail chewed on the bagel while thinking.

"You and I will team up, Tonto. I don't have Jeannie tagging along, so you will be stuck with me."

"Not a problem, Lone Ranger. Where do we start?"

"I want to quickly visit the first three crime scenes. No need to visit number four since I was there all morning. I just want to get a sense of each scene, something I learned from Jeannie. And, since your mind works like a damn computer, I will rely on you to keep tabs on my thought process. But I warn you, two plus two doesn't always add up to four with me or Jeannie."

Burk had a confused look on his face, "I don't understand."

"You will learn, my young grasshopper; you will learn."

20

CHAPTER

The snowfall had begun. It wasn't too heavy, but it was enough to make Rivas carefully consider his next move. He switched on the cab's heater, knowing the warmth might cause Tiffany to become drowsy sooner. As expected, she started yawning. "You seem tired. Why don't you hop in the back and get some rest? I'll continue driving for about an hour and then take a break at a rest area."

"I can't take your bed. I mean, you're driving me all the way to California. Where will you sleep?" Tiffany asked, concerned.

"Don't worry about me. When I reach the rest area, I'll be perfectly fine dozing off in my seat. After an hour, I'll be ready to hit the road again. I'll wake you up when we stop somewhere, and we can grab something to eat," Rivas assured her.

"If you're sure," Tiffany replied with a grateful smile on her face, assessing the easiest path to crawl into the sleeper area behind the driver and passenger seats. She lay on her stomach and slid onto the bed while Rivas enjoyed the sight. "Well, goodnight then," Tiffany said as she rolled over, facing away from Rivas.

Rivas anticipated that after about an hour, Tiffany would fall into a deep sleep, completely unaware of his intentions. He experienced an erection just thinking about how it would all play out.

Back in San Francisco, Ismail was astounded by the remarkable energy displayed by his team. Curious about the progress of the information flow, he approached Darcy, who responded with a confident smile and a thumbs-up.

Ismail and Burk drove to the three crime scenes. Burk eagerly took on the task of note-taking while Ismail vocalized his personal observations at each location. He meticulously pointed out the positions of surveillance cameras, the level of pedestrian activity, parked vehicles, and businesses that were either open or preparing to open during the time of the three murders. Burk struggled to keep pace with Ismail's rapid-fire commentary, diligently jotting down the information.

"I can't believe there were no witnesses," Ismail said. "It's crucial that we get access to the surveillance footage from all three locations. Make sure to check with the teams and find out if they've made any progress in obtaining it. There must be a missing link connecting the victims, God damn it," he added, frustration in his voice.

Retrieving a sheet of paper from their Epsom printer, Adam broke the silence. "We have our next target," he declared. Ariana, who had been seated at the kitchen table, rose from her chair and joined her brother near the couch. Placing the paper on the coffee table, Adam continued, "The guy's name is Peter Finch. I remember him from the trial, acting all self-righteous as if he hung onto every word spoken by the witness while he sat smugly in the jury box. Tonight, let's go out and start looking into Mr. Finch. How about ordering some take-out Chinese food?" As Ariana affectionately brushed her brother's hair off his shoulder, they prepared themselves for the task ahead.

Ismail was hard asleep at 7:45 on Saturday morning when his cell phone rang on the nightstand. His wife, who was cuddled up next to his back, stirred from her sleep and mumbled something about who was calling before turning over to the opposite side of the bed. "Dammit. Somebody's dead." Glancing at the caller ID, he confirmed it was Lomax on the line.

"Good morning, sir. I assume we have another case," Ismail greeted him.

"Damn, you're sharp. I don't understand why Jeannie thinks you're slow," Lomax replied.

Ismail couldn't contain his laughter, which erupted loudly. After regaining his composure, he inquired about the location of the crime scene.

"SFPD found a body near the water's edge close to the Presidio. If you head in that direction, you'll spot their cars. Also, I have a heads-up for you. A reliable source of mine called late last night and informed me that tomorrow's Sunday edition will feature the 'Number Killings' on the front page. It seems someone within the SFPD is leaking information. Be prepared for the press to start hounding you from today."

Ismail immediately dialed Burk's number and asked him to meet him at the crime scene. Anticipating the forensic team would require some time to arrive, Ismail placed a call to their supervisor requesting an expedited response. As he made his way to the location, a few blocks away, he could already spot the red and blue lights casting an eerie glow over the area despite the lingering fog that had yet to dissipate.

"Ismail, over here," called Jessie Thompson. "Man, your boss goes away, and bam, you get two new victims."

"Yeah, tell me about it. So, what do we have?" Ismail followed Thompson as they approached the water's edge, where a Latino male lay face up. The movement of his head was barely perceptible as each wave crashed against it. The rest of his body rested on broken concrete pieces that had been strategically placed to combat erosion.

Ismail's gaze focused on two entry wounds—one in the heart and another on the forehead. A red number '5' was etched just below the forehead wound, still visible despite most of the blood having been washed away, leading Ismail to assume it was made with a permanent marker once again.

"Our rookie officer over there was the first to arrive. Initially, he thought the victim had simply fallen, so he turned the body over. When he noticed the wounds, he immediately backed off, secured the area, and gave us a call. I knew it would be your jurisdiction even if it wasn't part of the serial killer investigation, so we stayed to help him preserve the scene until you guys showed up. By the way, do you have a new partner now that Jeannie's up in Idaho?" Thompson asked.

"Yeah, he should be arriving any minute now. Our forensic team is also on their way. If you could assign a few uniformed officers to keep any looky-loos at bay, that would be a great help. I'm guessing we don't have any witnesses?" Ismail asked, glancing around the area.

"No, unfortunately, we don't have any witnesses. Officer Gordon there was the only one present when he discovered the body. He had stepped out of his patrol car to stretch his legs and, while gazing out over the bay, spotted our unfortunate friend here. I'll request two day shift officers to stand here. Once they arrive, unless you specifically want to talk to Officer Gordon, I'll have him return to the station since his shift is over."

"No problem. Let him know that once another uniformed officer arrives, he's clear to head back to the station," Ismail replied, his focus still fixed on examining the body and surveying the crime scene.

"I'll tell him. Any progress on the other four homicides?" Jessie asked.

"No. We're still in the process of getting organized, but it's clear this killer is following a schedule, striking every seven days. We just need him to slip up once. Just once." Ismail's attention shifted as Burk arrived at the scene, and Ismail introduced him to Jessie.

As Thompson left and Burk looked at the body, Coroner Dr. Sally Brink arrived with an assistant at the same time as Linda Rivers, the FBI forensic team supervisor, and her team pulled up in their van. "Another one, Flo?" the coroner asked as soon as she saw Ismail.

"What can I say? I'm on a roll," came his reply. They proceeded to make their way down the embankment toward the body. Brink, with her handheld tape recorder in hand, led the way while her team followed closely behind, maintaining a short distance.

"The victim appears to be a middle-aged Latino male wearing a gray jogging suit," Brink reported into her handheld tape recorder. "There are two entrance wounds visible on the victim's forehead and heart regions. Surprisingly, there doesn't seem to be any noticeable effect from the seawater on the head area despite partial submersion. The jogging jacket appears wet, likely due to wave action. Rigor mortis has not set in. Additionally, there is a red number '5' on the victim's forehead."

Brink then directed one of her team members to take a liver temperature while she turned to Ismail. "Based on preliminary observations, it bears a resemblance to the case you had in the financial district. I won't state it officially just yet, but if I had to bet, my money would be on the same killer. The contusions on the body suggest that the victim was shot up there and then pushed down the embankment. I'll have more information for you once we complete the postmortem. Does tomorrow morning at ten work for you?"

Ismail nodded in agreement. "Tomorrow at ten sounds good. Let's reconvene then to discuss the findings in detail."

CHAPTER 21

Rivas sensed he was nearing the rest stop, a crucial point where he could unhitch his trailer and proceed down the interstate. Snow had just started to fall but was not heavy yet. The highway department had done a good job of clearing the interstate, but he hoped the turnout did not have too much snowpack yet.

The secluded turnout was a perfect hiding spot for his cab, where he could climb in the back with Tiffany and have his fun. His primary concern was ensuring she remained undisturbed during the disconnection process. Yet, even if she stirred awake, he planned to convince her that driving into the upcoming diner without the trailer would be more convenient, assuring her they would return for it later. The crucial element was to maintain her presence within the sleeping compartment.

Out of habit, he reached under his seat and touched the rope he would use. No need to knock her out since her fighting him was a turn-on. Fortunately, the rest stop was not very busy, and he found a spot away from other rigs and easily disconnected the trailer. He climbed back into the cab and found Tiffany still sound asleep.

A short time later, he spotted the turnoff. There was a fresh covering of snow, but nothing the cab could not handle. An hour later, it might be another story. He turned off the engine and gave the area a quick glance. Totally secluded. He grabbed the rope and climbed into the sleeper compartment.

Tiffany awoke as she felt Rivas moving into the sleeper compartment. She was startled. "Is everything alright?" she asked and then panicked when she saw the rope in Rivas' hand. Before she knew it, the rope was around her neck, and Rivas began choking her. She tried to fight him, but he was too strong. A short while later, she passed out. Rivas loosened the rope but kept it around her neck.

Rivas, satisfied that she was unconscious, removed her clothes, placing them in the corner of the sleeper. When he was through with her, he tightened the rope and applied pressure until he was sure she was dead. He put her sweater back on, as well as her pink panties. Like the others, he used the other end of the rope to tie her hands. He removed his condom and, after climbing from the sleeper into the driver's seat, threw it out of the window. Now, it was simply a choice of where to dump the body on the interstate. He needed a large snowpack.

At 7 a.m., Jeannie was already back at the substation, meticulously arranging items on the whiteboard. The previous night, she had realized that the overwhelming volume of data her team was dealing with was becoming nearly unmanageable. However, she was confident she had a solution in mind. By 7:30, Max arrived, followed by several other members of the task force.

"Good morning," Max greeted Jeannie, making immediate eye contact. "You're here bright and early."

"Yes, another restless night, as usual. My brain just won't shut off, no matter what I try," Jeannie replied with a sigh. "By the way, when does your Chief usually arrive?"

"He should be here any minute. Why do you ask?"

"I felt like we made significant progress yesterday, but as you can see from my stack of notes, the amount of information is staggering. We desperately need an IT specialist who can input it into a database and organize it. I have some ideas for today's priorities, but having a computer-savvy person on board would be incredibly helpful."

"Here he comes now," Max said, pointing towards the parking lot. They both observed the Chief stepping out of his private car and giving Jeannie's Corvette a scrutinizing look. "What an asshole. Most of us can't wait for him to retire."

"Well, let's give him a moment to settle into his office, and then I'll go down and butter him up to get us an IT person," Jeannie remarked, refocusing her attention on the whiteboard. "By the way, I hope you don't mind, but I need you to find a sandwich shop that can handle a large order. They can deliver it, or you can sneak out around 11:45 to pick it up," Jeannie continued. "Maybe a Subway or something similar would work. We'll also need drinks for everyone. Since we're dealing with a large group, it would be impractical to ask for individual preferences. Get some turkey, roast beef, ham, cheese, and so on. You can decide on the quantity, but I'd rather have leftovers than run out."

Jeannie had now become comfortable finding her way around the substation. She grabbed a cup of coffee and headed down to the Chief's office. She found him sitting at his desk, looking at a sporting magazine. When he saw her, he quickly closed the magazine, acting a little embarrassed.

"Agent Loomis. How goes the task force?" he asked, motioning her to take a chair across from his desk.

"After yesterday's session, it's clear that we're finally up and running. However, the sheer volume of information we've gathered so far is becoming a challenge to manage. That's why I came to see you,"

Jeannie explained, emphasizing the Chief's experience and rank in the department. "I was wondering if you could use your influence to find a skilled IT specialist who could create a comprehensive database for us to input all our information. It's crucial that this person understands the commitment required, as we'll need their expertise until we capture the killer. What are your thoughts?"

Jeannie wasn't particularly interested in the Chief's input on her request, but she understood the importance of playing the political game.

"Well," the Chief began to reply, "Considering the severity of this case and if I make a personal request, I believe we should be able to have a qualified person here by tomorrow. Will that be soon enough?"

Jeannie couldn't help but think to herself, "Pompous asshole." However, she maintained a broad smile on her face and expressed her gratitude, assuring the Chief that tomorrow would be perfect.

CHAPTER

Ismail gathered his team in the morning to discuss the progress they had made in identifying the gaps in the San Francisco Police Department's (SFPD) investigation into three homicides. He emphasized that their findings were not meant as criticism but rather a consequence of the defund the police movement. Sergeant Thompson from the SFPD had briefed them on the case, and now, it was up to Ismail's team to delve deeper and potentially shed light on the direction they should take to capture the killer.

Darcy had been busy inputting all the data they had gathered so far. Ismail hoped that by analyzing this information, they would gain insights into the next steps of their investigation. He instructed his team to continue exploring the SFPD's investigation, even if it meant starting from scratch as if they were assigned the case from the beginning.

Agent Susan Richards raised a question about the surveillance requests they had submitted. Ismail acknowledged her and explained that after dismissing the team, he and Burk would spend time reviewing the received surveillance material in hopes of finding something valuable. Ismail also assigned the task of reinterviewing family members, relatives, friends, and neighbors to uncover any crucial information or connections between the five victims. “Okay, people, let’s keep up the great work. Oh, plan on meeting back here at 4 p.m. so we can discuss our progress.”

After the team meeting, Ismail and Burk checked in with Darcy to see how she was progressing with the data input. Darcy informed them that she was almost done entering the information from the previous day, and once she incorporated the progress made by the teams that afternoon, she expected to have a printout ready for them by the following morning.

Curious about Jeannie’s investigation, Darcy asked Ismail if he had any updates from her. Ismail replied that he hadn’t heard anything but mentioned that he would give Jeannie a call in the evening to find out more and would let her know.

Burk and Ismail journeyed to the central Richmond district for a follow-up interview with the spouse of the fifth victim, Eddie Mays. As they approached her front door, Mrs. Mays, an elderly African American woman, greeted them. "Greetings, gentlemen from the FBI. I apologize for forgetting your names, but that doesn't matter. Please come inside and let me know if you have apprehended the wicked person who took my dear Eddie away."

Ismail noticed that Mrs. Mays appeared noticeably older since their last interview on the day her husband's body was discovered. Her gray hair was disheveled, and evidence of tears was visible. Ismail empathized with her deeply, particularly considering the absence of any suspects in custody.

"I regret to inform you, Mrs. Mays, that we haven't yet identified the individual responsible for your husband's tragic passing. However, I want to assure you that the entire San Francisco FBI Bureau is fully dedicated to this investigation. Agent Burk and I have a few additional questions we would like to ask you if you're feeling up to it."

"I'm willing to do anything I can to assist you two young officers. I'm not a vindictive person, but it was utterly wrong for someone to take my Eddie away from me. Only God possesses that authority. To shoot my Eddie while he was out for a jog ..." she paused, lost in her thoughts and shaking her head. Tears once again welled up and streamed down her face.

"During our previous conversation, you mentioned your husband usually drove to the Presidio for his jogging routine. Can you confirm if he followed this routine daily?"

"Oh, yes, indeed, God almighty, Eddie had a well-established routine that caught the attention of many. He followed a pattern of jogging every other day to accommodate the developing arthritis in his right knee. By taking a day off in between runs, he believed he could sustain his jogging regimen and stay in good shape. He would rise promptly at 5:30 a.m., enjoy a glass of orange juice and savor a slice of toast with butter and jelly. It seems those rituals brought him a sense of readiness for the day." Mrs. Mays smiled faintly but seemed lost in her thoughts once more.

Ismail inquired, "Mrs. Mays, I assume your husband was retired. Could you please share where he used to work?"

Mrs. Mays nodded and replied, "Eddie dedicated twenty-five years of his life working for the State of California. That's right. And you know, throughout all those years, he never took a sick day. Not even once. A mere cold couldn't keep my Eddie from fulfilling his duties."

Burk inquired, "Could you please share what his role was within the State of California?"

Mrs. Mays replied, "He worked for the Department of Motor Vehicles. I recall him coming home after work and entertaining the family with stories during dinner. He would recount incidents where he narrowly escaped danger while accompanying drivers on their test drives. You know, those individuals who were aiming to obtain their driver's licenses. Eddie had a knack for making the whole family burst into laughter with his tales."

"I apologize if my question may be sensitive, Mrs. Mays, but I must ask, did your husband have any individuals who harbored ill will towards him?" Ismail asked as delicately as he could.

"Eddie? No, sir. Everyone loved Eddie. You see, even after working hard all day, he would dedicate his time to coaching Little League. And when he wasn't coaching, he served as an umpire for the games. Eddie believed that the greatest enemy our black community faced was the challenges faced by young girls, with pregnancies out of wedlock and the absence of father figures at home.

He viewed his involvement with the youth, particularly those lacking a father figure, as a noble endeavor blessed by Jesus." Mrs. Mays became overwhelmed with emotion, her tears flowing uncontrollably as she reached for a box of tissues on the coffee table.

Burk asked, "Mrs. Mays, if we could focus on the last six months, did your husband's daily routine undergo any changes? In other words, did he have any negative encounters with anyone? Did he engage in arguments or display any unusual behavior?"

Ismail interjected, providing further context, "Mrs. Mays, if you've been following the news, it appears that your husband was a victim of a serial killer. Sadly, Mr. Mays was the fifth victim in this series of crimes. Our challenge, frankly, lies in establishing a connection between your husband and the other victims." Ismail produced a piece of paper displaying the driver's license photos and names of the four other individuals. "Are you familiar with any of these individuals?"

Mrs. Mays glanced at the photos but swiftly shook her head in a negative gesture. Ismail inquired, "So you're saying you've never encountered any of these individuals before?"

"No, what I meant is that my memory hasn't been reliable for nearly a year. It's not as sharp as my husband Eddie's. Could you provide me with a copy of these photos? My daughter is coming from San Jose today, and she can assist me in refreshing my memory. The same goes for your question about whether Eddie has changed any of his habits. I apologize for not being more helpful."

Ismail handed Mrs. Mays a copy of the photos and attached his business card with a paper clip given to him by Burk. He thought she might have lost the business card he had given her when he contacted her after her husband's murder. After completing this task, Ismail and Burk found their own way out.

They walked back to their bureau car, reflecting on the tough experience they had just encountered. Burk broke the silence by remarking, "Well, that was sobering."

Ismail nodded in agreement. "Yeah, it reminds me of something my dad used to say whenever a tragedy befell a decent family. He would shake his head and ask, 'Why do bad things always happen to good people and not vice versa?'"

The weight of the question lingered in the air as they reached their car, both deep in thought about the unfairness and unpredictability of life. They knew that their work, though challenging, was important in seeking justice and finding answers for those affected by such tragic events. With a renewed sense of determination, they got into the car and drove off, ready to continue their pursuit of truth and justice.

"We need to find this son-of-a-bitch, and when we do, I hope he resists," Ismail said as they headed to the bureau.

23

CHAPTER

Jeannie had just finished up the action items she had for her task force and was going to get her second or third cup of coffee. Max walked into the briefing room with a very attractive black woman, maybe in her mid to late twenties. "Jeannie, this is Sheila Floyd, our IT specialist."

Jeannie shook Sheila's hand and welcomed her on board. "I'm just heading for my umpteenth cup of coffee. Let me show you where everything is. I'm so glad you got here so soon. I'm afraid your work is going to be extensive."

As Jeannie and Sheila walked towards the coffee station, Jeannie began explaining the nature of the task force's work and the challenges they were facing. "Our task force has been dealing with a huge amount of data coming from twenty-one murders spread across five states, California, Oregon, Washington, Montana, and here in Idaho. We're hoping your expertise will help us tackle it effectively."

Sheila smiled and nodded, listening attentively. "Thank you, Jeannie. I'm excited to be here and ready to dive into the work. Could you give me a brief overview of the issue we're dealing with?"

Jeannie paused for a moment, considering how to summarize the situation succinctly. "Certainly," she replied, taking a sip of her coffee. Jeannie explained the need for a massive database that information from the twenty-one killings could be entered into and then have the computer system check for connections between the cases.

Sheila's eyes widened slightly, recognizing the gravity of the situation. "That sounds like a challenging task," she remarked. "Do we have any leads on who might be responsible?"

Jeannie shook her head, her expression filled with concern. "Unfortunately, no concrete leads yet. We suspect that the killer is a long-haul trucker using interstates as an easy way to escape after dumping his bodies. We are currently working backward from the most recent homicide to the previous one so that we can make an educated guess as to the route the suspect is taking."

Jeannie took Sheila aside and handed her the list she had prepared earlier. "Here are the specific requirements we need for our database setup," Jeannie explained. "We have a range of items, including a list of all interstates and known truck stops and rest areas, as well as the last known locations of the victims before their bodies were discovered. It's a comprehensive list, but it's crucial for our investigation."

Sheila carefully reviewed the list, nodding in understanding. "I'll make sure to incorporate all these elements into the database setup," she assured Jeannie. "I also have an idea for an algorithm that can help us predict his next move. Having a well-structured and organized system will significantly enhance our ability to analyze the data effectively."

Jeannie smiled appreciatively. "I have full confidence in your capabilities, Sheila. You remind me so much of my talented IT agent back in San Francisco. Take your time to familiarize yourself with our existing infrastructure and coordinate with the team members to gather any additional information you may need. We're all here to support you."

Sheila nodded, a determined look on her face. "Thank you, Jeannie. I'll get to work right away. Together, we'll strengthen our defenses and bring those responsible to justice."

With that, Sheila immersed herself in her new role, interacting with the team members, gathering information, and setting up the necessary database components. The task force was energized by her presence, knowing they had a skilled IT specialist on their side to tackle the challenges ahead. Jeannie watched the interaction between the investigators and then got up front and addressed her team.

"Alright, ladies and gentlemen, today is day five since the last reported body was found. The clock is ticking, but with the addition of Sheila, I feel confident that with the information I want you to start gathering today, we will close in on our killer.

Jeannie's words hung in the air as the task force members absorbed the gravity of the situation and the urgency and significance of the information they were tasked with gathering. Jeannie's logic resonated with them, and they recognized the importance of working backward from the most recent case to identify patterns and potential leads.

The room buzzed with a renewed sense of determination as each group began discussing their respective assignments. They organized themselves based on the states involved in the recent killings, ready to delve into details and compile the necessary data.

Jeannie approached the Idaho group, emphasizing the urgency of their task. "Idaho, as you have the most recent body drop, I need you to gather as much information as possible and provide it to Sheila right away," she directed. "Focus on the interstate and major highways that a trucker could have used to traverse the state. Additionally, compile the dates the victim's body was found and gather weather data for the day before and the day of the discovery. We need to establish any potential correlations."

The Idaho group nodded, fully grasping the importance of their role. They understood that their findings could serve as a crucial starting point for identifying connections between the victims and the truckers. They began discussing their plan of action, allocating tasks among themselves to ensure comprehensive coverage.

Meanwhile, the other groups took note of their assignments and started dividing responsibilities accordingly. Each group would focus on their respective states, researching the road networks and compiling information about the victims, including their backgrounds, any indications of them being runaways, and possible motivations for getting in a truck with a stranger.

Jeannie continued addressing the various teams, emphasizing the need for thoroughness and attention to detail. "Remember, we're not just gathering data; we're also looking for patterns, motives, and potential links between the victims and truckers," she reminded them. "Document everything meticulously and keep open lines of communication with each other and Sheila. Collaboration is key to our success."

Jeannie concluded the briefing with an inspiring message. "We're making progress, and I have full confidence in each and every one of you. Let's work together, support Sheila, and push forward with determination. Time is of the essence, and we will not rest until we've solved this case and put an end to this killer's reign of terror."

With a shared sense of purpose, the task force members became fully engaged in their assignments. They knew their actions could be the key to stopping the killer and bringing closure to the victims' families. As they dove into their work, the room buzzed with a palpable energy fueled by a collective commitment to succeed.

Jeannie stood at the front of the room, looking at the tired yet determined faces of her team members. She recognized their hard work and dedication and knew they deserved a break. With gratitude in her voice, she addressed the task force.

"Thank you all for your exceptional effort today," Jeannie began. "I see the long hours you've put in, and I'm truly grateful for your commitment to this investigation. You've made significant progress, and we're moving in the right direction."

She paused for a moment, allowing her words to sink in. "I want to give you all a chance to rest and recharge. Tomorrow morning, we'll start a bit later, at 9 a.m., and we'll have the initial catering crew serving breakfast. You deserve a good night's sleep and a chance to lie in a bit."

A wave of relief washed over the tired faces in the room. Smiles appeared, and the atmosphere lightened. Jeannie's considerate gesture was well-received by the team, knowing that their efforts were valued.

"I know this case is demanding, and we're dealing with high stakes," Jeannie continued, "But taking care of ourselves is just as important as the work we're doing. So, get a good night's sleep, recharge your batteries, and come back tomorrow refreshed and ready to tackle the challenges ahead."

The team members nodded appreciatively, with gratitude evident in their eyes. They knew Jeannie understood the importance of balance in such intense investigations. With a final word of encouragement, Jeannie concluded, "Thank you again, everyone. You're doing exceptional work, and I'm proud to have each of you on this team. Rest up, enjoy your evening, and I'll see you all tomorrow morning at 9 a.m."

As the task force members filed out of the briefing room, there was a renewed sense of energy. They looked forward to a well-deserved break and the prospect of a fresh start the next day. The promise of breakfast and a delayed start time added a touch of anticipation, allowing them to momentarily set aside the weight of the investigation and focus on self-care.

Jeannie watched as her team members left, feeling a deep sense of appreciation for their dedication. She knew this temporary respite would help reenergize them for the challenges that lay ahead. With a hopeful smile, she looked forward to reconvening with her team, ready to continue the pursuit of justice in the morning. Before leaving, she checked in on Sheila, who was so engrossed in her computer that she didn't hear Jeannie enter her office.

"Hey, girl, I sent the team home. You need to get some sleep, and we will meet back here at 9 a.m. for breakfast."

"Oh, okay, Jeannie. I think you are going to like what I envision, but you're right; I am exhausted." She closed her laptop, grabbed her purse, and left the substation with Jeannie.

"Thanks again for requesting me," she said before entering her vehicle and leaving the parking lot.

24

CHAPTER

Ismail and Burk returned to the bureau feeling a bit frustrated as they believed their conversation with Mrs. Mays had been unproductive. "You know, Flo," Burk began, "Last night, Darcy and I were discussing the ……." He suddenly halted and blushed. He had unintentionally made a Freudian slip and revealed that he and Darcy were involved in a romantic relationship.

Ismail couldn't help but laugh at the awkwardness of the moment. "Don't worry, Burk. The fact that you and Darcy are together is the worst-kept secret in the entire bureau. In fact, everyone believes you make a great couple."

Burk, still blushing and needing a few moments to compose himself, came to terms with the fact that everyone was aware of his intimate relationship with Darcy. Collecting his thoughts, he continued the conversation. "You know how Darcy and I are both analytical. Well, we sat down and created two columns on a piece of paper last night. From our perspective, there are two possibilities for these murders.

On one hand, the killing could be entirely random. There may be no connection between the victims, so attempting to establish one would be futile. However, it's a necessary task, even though the outcome might be inconclusive."

Ismail listened attentively, trying his best to suppress another laugh at the mental image of Burk and Darcy doing the dirty together. He tried to remain focused regarding Burk and Darcy's synopsis of the investigation.

Burk pressed on, determined to present his and Darcy's perspective. "However, there is, indeed, a connection among the victims, and we believe that is the key to cracking this case. Out of the two possibilities, this approach holds more promise. I understand that you've already explored both options, and it feels foolish to bring it up again, but Darcy thinks that if she could delegate the data input to another computer assistant, she could concentrate on developing a program that could quickly identify any kind of correlation, potentially saving us a significant amount of time."

"Damn, Burk. Whatever it takes," Ismail replied emphatically. "Do you and Darcy have anyone specific in mind for the job? I'll arrange for their transfer here as soon as possible."

"Actually, she is in our bureau. Susan Richards. She has a degree in computer science and is a wiz with computers. She could start immediately."

"Really? Consider it done," Ismail responded eagerly. He dialed Agent Richards' number on his cell phone, instructing her to put aside her current tasks and join forces with Darcy. The two of them would now be working together as a team. "Great job, grasshopper," Ismail added, intentionally leaving his comment hanging in the air to tease Burk a little. "Oh, and when you see Darcy," he continued, "pass along the message that I spoke with Jeannie last night. She believes the task force is getting closer to identifying the suspect up there."

As they made their way through the congested traffic, Ismail and Burk sat in silence, lost in their thoughts. Ismail's mind wandered back to his late-night conversation with Jeannie. They had engaged in their usual playful banter before Jeannie began describing the direction her task force had taken in their investigation. Ismail couldn't help but feel confident that Jeannie would succeed in solving her serial case long before he would his own.

Ismail proceeded to provide Jeannie with a detailed account of their ongoing investigation. Jeannie listened attentively, occasionally interjecting with insights on the matter, but for the most part, allowing Ismail to outline the avenues they were exploring. When Ismail concluded, he eagerly inquired about her thoughts.

"You're absolutely right. If the victims are truly random and unrelated, it will be an incredibly challenging case to solve, as we both know. However, if luck is on your side and you manage to identify a common denominator among them, you'll crack this case swiftly." She paused momentarily before continuing, "By the way, your investigation has garnered attention up here as well. They're calling it the 'Numbers Killer' case in the news. Have you been keeping Thompson updated on your progress?"

"Nah, things have been quite hectic," Ismail admitted. "I moved Susan Richards in with Darcy. She is supposed to be a computer wiz, and it should definitely help streamline the process. Hopefully, Darcy can work her magic with the additional support."

Ismail took a moment to gather his thoughts before continuing, "You're right about the timeline. The killer seems to have a consistent pattern of striking every seven days. It's as if this frequency holds some significance or necessity for them. It could be a vital clue we need to unravel."

"Let me ask you something," Jeannie said as if she was still formulating her thoughts. "Have you considered the killer being a female? At least think about it. Let's say the killer's motivation is revenge for something. As you know, revenge is a primary motivation for women murdering a husband or boyfriend."

Ismail was intrigued by Jeannie's question and the possibility she presented. "That's an interesting thought, boss," he responded. "While we haven't ruled out any possibilities, we have been primarily focusing on male suspects due to certain profiling indicators. Do you have any specific reasons or insights that make you lean towards the killer being female?"

"No. And I'm not saying with any specificity that your killer is female. Just thinking out loud about revenge possibly being a factor. Hell, it could be a team of killers. Who knows?"

As Ismail processed Jeannie's insights, her reference to similar cases involving female perpetrators during her time at the BAU intrigued him. The notion of revenge as a potential motivation also struck a chord. He couldn't help but acknowledge the possibility that the killer in their current case might, indeed, be female.

"Huh," Ismail responded, still contemplating Jeannie's input. "You raise some valid points, boss. While I won't jump to conclusions, it's worth considering the possibility of a female suspect. Revenge as a motivation does align with certain characteristics commonly associated with female offenders."

He paused for a moment before continuing, "You're right. I should widen the scope of our investigation. It's crucial not to dismiss any potential avenues. Although the idea of a team of killers might be a stretch, we shouldn't entirely rule out any possibilities at this stage. Thank you, boss lady. I appreciate your insights."

Back at the bureau, Ismail gathered his entire team, including Darcy and Richards. As everyone settled in, Ismail looked at each team member, capturing their attention. "I had a conversation with Jeannie last night," he began, maintaining a deliberate pause for effect. "First, she sends her greetings and wants you all to know that our investigation has made it to the front page of the local Idaho papers and has garnered attention on television channels as well. She also brought up a couple of crucial points for us to consider."

The team members leaned in, eager to hear Jeannie's insights. Excitement and anticipation filled the room. "One thing we need to consider is the possibility of the suspect being a female," Ismail announced. Instantly, chatter erupted among the team members as they exchanged thoughts and opinions. Ismail allowed them a few moments to crosstalk before continuing.

"Additionally, Jeannie mentioned that we should keep an open mind and consider the outside chance that we might be dealing with a team of killers," Ismail added, noticing the talk among the agents intensifying. The room buzzed with a mix of curiosity and heightened focus as the team contemplated these new possibilities. "So, keep these possibilities in the back of your minds while you conduct your interviews."

With that, Ismail released the team, hoping that by the end of the day, they might uncover something, anything, that could provide the breakthrough they desperately needed in the case.

Later, as Ismail settled into Jeannie's office, now temporarily his, he remembered her inquiry about whether he had kept Sergeant Thompson, her latest romantic interest, in the loop. He reached for the phone and dialed the number for the San Francisco Police Department's Homicide Division. Thompson picked up on the third ring.

"Thompson, it's Flores," Ismail greeted him. "I don't have a whole lot to share regarding the five killings. Today marks day three since the last murder. I suppose, if it's any solace, we have four more days to capture this guy, that's if he continues with his normal pattern."

CHAPTER 25

Jeannie's cell phone vibrated on her nightstand at 4:15 in the morning, startling her awake. Not recognizing the caller ID, she answered cautiously, "Loomis."

"Jeannie, it's Max. We have another one," came the voice on the other end. Jeannie's heart sank. The time between kills was narrowing. They agreed to meet at the substation, and from there, Max would provide transportation using a department's four-wheeler, considering the steady snowfall throughout the night. Jeannie was extra cautious as she drove her sports car to the substation, grateful that the road crew had cleared the main roads.

Upon arriving, Jeannie spotted the four-wheeler and parked her Corvette in her normal spot. She climbed into the patrol vehicle, relieved to feel the warmth of the heater chasing away the chill of the early morning.

"So, what do we have?" Jeannie asked, settling in beside Max.

"Based on the information I received from dispatch and the initial officer at the scene, it appears to be a Snow Angel case," Max explained. "The victim is a white female with a rope around her neck and her hands tied. She has blond hair and is estimated to be in her late twenties or early thirties." The grim details painted a haunting picture of another tragic murder.

"Okay, have you notified the coroner?" Jeannie inquired, focused on the necessary procedures ahead.

"Not yet," Max replied. "I wanted to wait and see how you wanted to proceed."

"Good," Jeannie nodded. "I want to personally inspect the scene before it becomes crowded. Hold off on calling in the forensic team as well, and let's minimize radio communication. The last thing we need is the press showing up and jeopardizing the investigation."

As they approached the crime scene, Jeannie couldn't help but notice the eerie similarity to the crime scene photos she had seen from the previous cases. Nearly 70% of the body drops had occurred on snowbanks. Jeannie shared her observation with Max, explaining that it indicated the killer's primary hunting grounds were in snowy regions. However, the other instances where bodies were found lying on the side of the road suggested that the killer was venturing into different areas where there was no snow.

"What do you mean?" Max inquired, intrigued by Jeannie's assessment.

"My intuition tells me that the killer's main routes take him through regions of the five states where snow is prevalent for a significant part of the year," Jeannie explained. "Those bodies found in areas without snow indicate that he's still employing the same killing method, but he's driving and operating outside his comfort zone, away from the snowy areas."

"I never thought about that," Max admitted, realizing the significance of Jeannie's observation. As they arrived at the scene, Jeannie noticed two other patrol units already present, their emergency lights flashing.

"Hey guys," Jeannie called out to the officers. "Do me a favor and shut off your emergency lights. I want each of you positioned at different points along the road. One down there and one up there." She pointed in opposite directions. "When you see headlights of approaching vehicles, flag them down and wait until I give the clear signal for them to pass. Understood?" Both officers nodded, indicating their understanding of the instructions.

The lights on the patrol units were switched off, leaving the area in a somber darkness. Jeannie proceeded to assess the crime scene, aware of the need for a thorough investigation and careful preservation of evidence. The snow-covered surroundings added an eerie backdrop to the tragic event that had unfolded there.

From her vantage point, the snow angel appeared just like the previous victims. Serene. Peaceful. The victim's long blond hair cascaded around her angelic face, creating a poignant contrast with the grim reality of her demise. Jeannie approached the body, careful not to disturb the scene. Jeannie pulled a pair of gloves from her pocket and put them on.

As Jeannie observed the lifeless body of the young woman, her mind began to wander to the future, filled with thoughts of the eventual capture of the ruthless killer. She couldn't help but consider the media frenzy that would follow, unknowingly making him a twisted celebrity in the eyes of the public. The prospect of years of court battles and endless discussions by television pundits weighed heavily on her.

In the depths of her frustration and anger, a thought crossed Jeannie's mind—a dark thought that reflected her deepest desire for justice. She contemplated the idea of the killer receiving the ultimate punishment—a swift and final bullet to the head. While such thoughts were fleeting and only whispered within her own mind, they revealed the depths of her determination to bring this perpetrator to justice and ensure that no more innocent lives would be lost.

She tried unsuccessfully to suppress these dark musings, but thoughts of the victims and their grieving families deserved nothing less than the full force of justice to be brought down upon the killer, ensuring that he would never have the opportunity to harm again.

A thought came to Jeannie. She turned to Max. "My flashlight is not very strong. Do you have something better in the car?"

"Yeah, let me go get it," he replied.

As Max turned to retrieve a stronger flashlight from his car, Jeannie seized a momentary opportunity. With a swift motion, she carefully plucked a few strands of the victim's hair from her scalp. Quick and discreet, she ensured no trace of her actions would be detected. Slipping off her right glove, Jeannie tucked the hair strands securely inside and placed the makeshift evidence container in her pocket. From her left front pocket, she retrieved a pair of leather gloves, seamlessly replacing the ones she had previously worn. Max, unaware of the subtle switch, returned with the improved flashlight.

Jeannie cast a final glance at the lifeless snow angel, taking mental note of the scene. With a purposeful stride, she walked back up to Max and instructed him to contact the coroner and the forensics team.

After the exchange with the coroner, which yielded no significant new insights, Max drove Jeannie back to the substation. They wasted no time in briefing the Chief upon his arrival. Jeannie sensed his growing frustration with what he perceived as a lack of progress in the investigation, and she couldn't help but share some of that sentiment.

As they presented the latest findings and discussed the challenges they faced, the Chief's impatience was palpable. The pressure to solve the case weighed heavily on everyone involved, and Jeannie understood the urgency of the situation. However, she also knew that rushing to hasty conclusions could compromise the thoroughness of their investigation.

"Chief, we're doing everything we can to make progress," Jeannie assured him, her voice conveying a mix of determination and empathy. "However, we're dealing with a cunning killer who leaves little trace. It's going to take time to connect the dots and gather the evidence we need. We can't afford to overlook any detail or make premature assumptions."

The Chief, though visibly frustrated, seemed to absorb Jeannie's words. He knew she was right, and, deep down, he recognized the dedication and expertise of her team. With a sigh, he nodded and said, "Alright, keep pushing forward. We need a breakthrough soon."

Jeannie and Max left the Chief's office, their minds focused on the task at hand. Up rushed an excited Sheila. "Jeannie, I may have something." They followed Sheila back to her tiny office where, on a table, she had a printout of the various interstates that traversed California, Oregon, Washington, Montana, and Idaho.

"Let me bring it up on the computer; it's easier for me to manipulate the data and overlay the material."

CHAPTER 26

Sheila brought up a map showing all five states. "Let's start with the two most recent cases here in Idaho." Colored lines highlighted the various interstates. "As you can see, there's nothing earth-shattering here. Two red lines indicate the most probably used roadway. Now, working backward, we have the next three killings." Blue lines showed the possible routes but also overlaps connecting the two from the Idaho cases.

"Son-of-a-bitch," Max said, focused on the computer screen. Jeannie had a huge smile on her face while looking at Sheila.

"Good work. Max, grab a car. We need to take a ride to all known truck stops in both directions of this morning's body drop. We're closing in. I can feel it."

About forty-five minutes later, they arrived at a large truck stop illustrated by the huge number of big rigs in the parking lot. "My dad always used to say that if you saw a bunch of truckers stopped at a restaurant, it guaranteed two things: Good food and plenty of it," Jeannie said as she climbed out of the patrol vehicle.

"How do you want to handle this?" Max asked.

"First, I will ask to see the manager and get permission to view the surveillance tapes. If that doesn't yield anything, then we can sample their food and head to the next stop."

Jeannie and Max entered the bustling truck stop, the aroma of coffee and freshly cooked food wafting through the air. They made their way toward the manager's office, passing truckers engrossed in their meals and conversations. Jeannie couldn't help but feel a sense of determination and anticipation as they approached a potential lead in their investigation.

"Good afternoon, sir," Jeannie greeted the manager with a friendly smile as they entered his office. "I'm Special Agent Jeannie Loomis, and this is Detective Elders of the State Police. We're currently working on an ongoing investigation, and we wondered if we could have access to your surveillance tapes for the past few days."

"You're working the Snow Angel case?" he asked sarcastically. Neither Jeannie nor Max replied. The manager, an obese middle-aged man with a worn-out expression, nodded in response. "Sure, Agent Loomis, Detective Elders. You have a search warrant?"

Jeannie looked at Max and smiled. She turned her attention to the manager. "Look. We are working a major investigation. Now, we have two ways to proceed. You can give your permission and cooperate like an upright citizen eagerly wanting to assist with law enforcement, or I can shut this place down until we get a search warrant. And since it is a Friday, the judge is probably going to be hard to locate, so that might take hours, don't you think, Detective?"

"You can't shut me down. Friday through Sunday nights are our busiest crowds. Why would you need to do that?"

"Well, we don't know how much evidence collection we might need, and we can't allow people, including you, to destroy evidence, even if it is not intentional."

Sweat began to appear on the manager's forehead. "Alright. Come with me, and I will show you our surveillance setup. The two followed the manager to the back of the small grocery store attached to the main diner.

"Let me pull up the footage for you," he said as Jeannie winked at Max. He quickly navigated through the computer system and brought up the relevant recordings. The trio watched intently as the surveillance footage revealed the truck stop's comings and goings.

"I feel comfortable managing your equipment. Could you leave my partner and me alone due to the confidentiality of the case?" Jeannie asked, not expecting a negative response. Disappointedly, the manager left the room.

As they reviewed the tapes, they paid close attention to any suspicious or unusual activity. Time seemed to stretch as they meticulously analyzed each frame, searching for any signs that could link the killer to the truck stop.

After several minutes of watching, Max suddenly pointed at the screen. "Wait! Rewind that," he said, his voice filled with excitement. Jeannie obliged, rewinding the footage, and they watched it again. This time, they noticed a trucker watching someone talking on the phone inside the small grocery store attached to the café.

Jeannie switched to footage from inside the grocery store. "Damn! It's our victim!" she excitedly said. "Right down to the sweater she was wearing when we found her this morning."

They continued to watch. As the victim continued to talk on the phone, the possible suspect entered the store and bought a few items, but always in an area where he could eavesdrop on her conversation. He quickly paid for a few items and timed his exit to that of the victim. They appeared to have a brief conversation, where the victim seemed relaxed, even laughing at times. The two walked to a tractor-trailer rig, and he helped her into the cab. Jeannie and Max noted that he had parked his rig in a relatively secluded area away from the other trucks.

Jeannie's smile grew wider. "We've got him," she said, her voice tinged with excitement. "Let's see if we can get a closer look at his truck. Here's the plate. Write it down so we can run it later," Jeannie instructed Max.

Max quickly jotted down the license plate number that Jeannie provided, ensuring they had the necessary information to run a thorough check on the truck and its owner. He shared Jeannie's excitement, realizing that they had potentially achieved a major breakthrough in their investigation.

"Absolutely, Jeannie. We've got a solid lead here," Max replied, his voice filled with anticipation. "Let's document everything and make sure we have all the evidence we need. This could be the break we've been waiting for."

"We need to find out who this guy is and get a closer look at his truck," Jeannie emphasized, her determination evident. "Let's document this footage and secure the evidence. I will tell the manager to save all gas receipts starting during this period. We need to proceed with caution. We don't want to tip him off."

It seemed to take forever to get back to the substation. Both had forgotten about sitting down for a meal at the truck stop. There'd be plenty of time to eat once the asshole was in custody. Jeannie gave the good news to the task force members. Quickly, they identified that the tractor-trailer rig was part of a large fleet owned by the Pacific Coast shipping company with an office in Boise.

The realization that the suspect had been operating within their own jurisdiction all along sent a wave of disbelief through the team. It was a stark reminder that evil could lurk anywhere, even close to home. Jeannie couldn't help but feel a mix of frustration and relief. They had been tirelessly searching for the Snow Angel killer, unaware that he had been right under their noses.

"We never suspected he was operating so close to us," Jeannie commented, her voice tinged with a hint of frustration. "But now, we have an advantage. We know his whereabouts, and we can move swiftly to apprehend him."

She had her team focus their efforts on gathering more information about the suspect and his potential connections to the Pacific Coast shipping company. They coordinated with law enforcement agencies and planned their next steps to ensure a seamless operation.

Jeannie addressed the team, her voice steady but resolute. "We have the advantage of local knowledge and resources. Let's use that to its fullest. Coordinate with the Pacific Coast shipping company and gather as much information as possible about the suspect and his movements. We need to close in on him swiftly and decisively."

The team members nodded, fully aware of the gravity of the situation. The case had become intensely personal to them all, fueled by a desire to protect their community from further harm. As they prepared for the final stages of their operation, Jeannie's mind raced with thoughts of the victims and their families. She couldn't shake off the weight of responsibility that rested on their shoulders. It was up to them to bring closure and justice to those affected by the Snow Angel killer's reign of terror.

She concluded, addressing her team with three words, "This ends now."

27

CHAPTER

Ariana received a text message to check her email. Her curiosity was piqued as she examined the picture of Jose Aguilera. Memories of the trial flooded back, and she recalled the details surrounding his involvement. The email provided additional information about Jose, including his age and residence in the Castro District, a neighborhood known for its vibrant LGBTQ+ community.

"Hmm, seems like he might be gay," Ariana thought to herself, considering the demographics of that area. While it was a generalization to assume someone's sexual orientation based on their place of residence, the neighborhood's reputation as an LGBTQ+ hub added an interesting layer to the scenario.

Adam arrived home from shopping, and his sister showed him the paper she had printed out of their latest victim. "This one's yours," she said, handing him the picture and some pertinent information about where he worked and home address. "He wants us to kill him tomorrow instead of waiting seven days. He doesn't say why, but since you are up, let's check on him right after we have a snack. Let's take the gun. We might luck out and be able to make the hit today."

"Are you sure? Normally, we spend some time watching their movements and then select a time and location," Adam replied.

"Look, the cops have their heads so far up their asses, they have no leads whatsoever. Some of those houses in the Castro district have single-car garages. We might luck out and spot him coming home, and when he drives into his garage, bang."

They found his house easily and set up down the street watching his house. Using her cell phone, Ariana called the residence, but no one answered. She then called his cell phone number. He answered. She knew that if he had glanced at his caller ID, it would show unknown. She hung up. "Well, he's out somewhere. If the information we got is correct, and he works a 9-5 job, we only have about a half-hour to waste. You better scoot over towards me so we look like a pair of horny assholes making out."

Apparently, no one cared about them being present since no cops arrived to harass them. Forty-one minutes later, they saw a red Volkswagen slow down as the garage of the residence they were watching slowly rose. Adam took the .22 revolver out of the glove box and placed it in his right front pocket. "Be back in a second," he said, with a smile on his face.

He walked up to the garage at a brisk pace. Jose was getting out of the car. "Hey, Jose," Adam said. As Jose tried to focus on the male standing next to him, two shots entered his body. One in the chest and one in the head. Adam pulled out his red marker and wrote '5' on Jose's still-warm forehead, then turned and walked calmly back to his ride.

Ismail was eating a deli sandwich he and Burk picked up on the way back to the bureau after visiting number two's neighbors, which had yielded nothing. As he was about to take another bite of his sandwich, his cell phone rang. He did not recognize the number.

"Agent Flores," he stated.

"Agent Flores, I'm Eddie Mays' daughter, Lucy Williams. I'm calling on behalf of my mother."

"Oh, yes. Thank you for calling me back. Hang on just one minute." He wiped mustard and mayonnaise from his mustache and grabbed a paper napkin to write down any worthwhile notes.

"Okay. Was your mother able to recall anything regarding the paper I left with several photos?"

"No. Sorry. She really concentrated on them but said she had never seen them before."

"Thank you for checking with your mother. I appreciate your help," Ismail replied, his tone filled with determination but also frustration. "If she remembers anything about them or any other information that might be relevant, please don't hesitate to reach out." Ismail was about ready to hang up the phone and go back to attacking his sandwich.

"Agent Flores, are you still there?"

"Yes, I'm still here," Ismail replied.

"As I was helping my mom remember, you know, while looking at the photos, she said you asked her if my dad's daily routine had changed in the last several days."

"Ms. Williams, what I was inquiring about is if your mom could remember anything in your dad's routine that had changed over the last couple of months. She said she needed you to help her with her memory."

"Yes. I reminded her that about nine months ago, my father had to serve as a juror. My dad wasn't like most of us, who would try anything to get out of jury duty. He felt it was his duty. Anyway, he sat on the jury for almost two weeks. His only regret was not being able to jog during that time. I don't know if that helps, but we wanted you to know."

"Do you know what type of case he served as a juror?"

Ms. Williams whispered into the phone, obviously not wanting her mother to hear what she was about to reveal. "It was a child molestation case. The accused was apparently enticing children to get in his car, where he fondled them and, well, you know," her voice trailed off.

"Thank you, Ms. Williams. Your information is valuable to our investigation," Ismail responded, a spark of hope rekindling within him. "Please convey our gratitude to your mother as well. We truly appreciate her cooperation and willingness to help. I will make sure to follow up on this lead and see if we can establish any connection," Ismail continued, his voice filled with renewed determination. "If we find anything further or need to clarify any details, I'll be sure to reach out to you."

With a sense of urgency, Burk swiftly made his way through the bureau, calling each team member and relaying Ismail's message. The excitement was contagious, and the team quickly assembled in the briefing room, anticipation filling the air.

Ismail came racing out of the men's restroom, almost colliding with Lomax. "Oh, sorry, sir. We have a major break in the case. I'm on my way to the briefing room if you care to join."

"Absolutely," he replied as the two hurriedly made their way down the hallway.

As Ismail entered the room, his eyes gleaming with determination, the team members turned their attention towards him. Ismail wasted no time and dove right into the newfound breakthrough.

"Team, we may have just stumbled upon a crucial lead," Ismail began, his voice filled with energy. "All four victims served on jury duty, including Eddie Mays. It turns out he served for about two weeks, approximately nine months ago, on a molestation case. Unfortunately, we don't have more details due to his widow's memory problems. But this connection is significant."

Susan, still processing the information, spoke up, "I have access to court records and databases. I can dig deeper and find out the specifics of the case Eddie Mays was a juror on. It may take some time, but I'll do my best to uncover any relevant details."

Ismail turned to Darcy, who had a satisfied smile on her face. "Darcy, you've already done remarkable work. Your algorithm found the connection between all four victims. We need you to continue tapping into jury selection records and gather as much information as possible. We're counting on you."

Darcy nodded, her fingers already flying across the keyboard, determined to retrieve the necessary data. "I'll do my best, Ismail. I'll cross-reference the names of the victims and gather all the pertinent information. We'll have a clearer picture of what we're dealing with." With the team fired up and their expertise aligned, Ismail felt a surge of confidence. The pieces of the puzzle were finally starting to come together, and they were closing in on the truth.

"Let's reconvene in one hour with all the information we've gathered," Ismail instructed, his voice carrying the weight of their progress. "This is a breakthrough, and it's crucial that we work swiftly but thoroughly. We owe it to the victims and their families to bring justice."

As the team started to disperse, Ismail added one additional instruction. "Let's keep this lead close to the vest. Right now, it is all we have. We are racing against the clock with four days remaining before he is due to kill again."

While walking back to his office, Lomax's cell phone rang. "Lomax," he said. "One minute. I'm almost back to my office." As soon as he finished the phone call, he grabbed the notes he had taken and quickly went to Jeannie's office, where he found Ismail and Burk.

"You've got another one," he said matter of factly.

Ismail's hand trembled slightly as he took the paper from Lomax, his heart sinking at the realization that the killer had struck again, deviating from his established pattern. He quickly scanned the information, his mind racing to process the new details.

"Damn it, he's accelerating," Ismail muttered, his voice laced with frustration. "We can't afford to waste any time. Burk, gather the team immediately. We need to analyze the new crime scene and gather as much evidence as possible, especially his identification. We'll call it into Darcy and Susan and have them check to see if he, too, was a juror."

28

CHAPTER

Jeannie's mind raced as she absorbed the information about the Pacific Coast Shipping Company. The magnitude of their operations became evident, and it posed a significant challenge to their investigation. She knew that to uncover any potential leads or connections, they would need to delve deep into the company's structure and operations.

"Alright, team," Jeannie addressed her task force members gathered in the briefing room. "We have a massive task ahead of us. The Pacific Coast Shipping Company is a sprawling organization, with its corporate office located in Los Angeles and numerous sub-agencies spread across all five states. Additionally, there are smaller offices servicing each rig after a run." She paused, scanning the faces of her team, seeing a mixture of determination and concern. They understood the complexity of the situation and the magnitude of the investigation.

"Our goal is to thoroughly analyze their records discretely. We don't want to tip off our suspect." Jeannie assigned specific tasks to her team members, leveraging their individual strengths and areas of expertise.

"California," Jeannie emphasized, find the exact location of the corporation and arrange to have an agency contact them, again, discretely, and find out who was driving the rig with these plates yesterday. You guys have local knowledge and connections that could be invaluable to our investigation. I feel he is either making a run for home or getting ready to turn in his rig."

Jeannie pondered the situation, realizing that while the focus of the investigation shifted to the Pacific Coast Shipping Company and Idaho, her teams representing Oregon, Washington, and Montana didn't have an immediate role in those aspects. It was crucial to keep her team engaged and involved, ensuring they remained an integral part of the overall investigation.

"Alright, for my teams from Oregon, Washington, and Montana, while the primary focus is on the Pacific Coast Shipping Company and the Idaho substation, we can't afford to overlook any potential leads in the other regions. I want you to dig deeper into the backgrounds of the victims, specifically looking for reasons our victims might have decided to hitch a ride with our suspect. Without revealing our latest lead and how it appears our suspect picks up stray women on his route, find out why your victims were seeking a ride, so to speak."

The Oregon, Washington, and Montana teams re-examined witness statements, interviewed friends and family members, and scrutinized any relevant information that could shed light on the victims' movements and encounter with the suspect.

"I want you to think outside the box," Jeannie continued, her voice filled with determination. "We need to consider any possible angles or connections that could tie these cases together. Look deeper into their personal lives. Did they come from broken homes? Were they runaways seeing a better life somewhere?"

Stay in close communication with the other teams and exchange information. We're looking for connections in our victims' behavior and why that connection drove them into the path of the killer."

About an hour later, Max quickly entered the briefing room. "There's an associated truck agency right here in Coeur d'Alene, about five miles from here."

"Are you kidding me?" Jeannie asked as she grabbed her purse, and the two headed to his patrol vehicle.

As Jeannie and Max rushed to the car, the realization of a potential breakthrough sent a surge of anticipation through both. The proximity of an associated truck agency in Coeur d'Alene, just five miles away, raised the possibility of finding a crucial lead in their investigation.

They quickly got into the vehicle, and Jeannie buckled her seatbelt while Max started the engine. As they sped off toward the truck agency, their minds raced with hope. The proximity of the agency meant they could potentially uncover valuable evidence or gather information that could bring them closer to the killer.

Jeannie checked her phone, ensuring she had all the relevant case files and information at her fingertips. She was prepared to question employees, examine records, and gather any evidence that might tie the agency to the crimes. Max focused on driving, maneuvering through the traffic with a sense of urgency, and understanding the significance of their mission.

The journey to the associated truck agency felt both brief and endless, as every second counted in their pursuit of the truth. As they pulled into the agency's parking lot, Jeannie and Max exchanged a determined glance, ready to face whatever awaited them inside.

"Let's go," Jeannie said, her voice filled with resolve. They exited the vehicle, adrenaline coursing through their veins, and made their way towards the agency's entrance. It was time to gather information on the rig's driver and, with luck, find evidence in his cab if he turned it in.

They were greeted by a receptionist as they entered the office. They could see through a window several cabs being washed. Urgently, after identifying herself, Jeannie requested to see the manager. The manager arrived wearing a blue shirt with his name and title. Jeannie again showed her badge and asked if there was someplace private. Once in his office, Jeannie showed him a printout of the registration information for the cab seen in the surveillance footage. She asked if this particular cab had recently been brought in or checked out. The officer typed the information into his computer and turned the screen so Jeannie and Max could read it.

"The cab was, indeed, brought in early this morning," the manager confirmed. "The driver who checked it in was James Rivas. We have his date of birth and driver's license number, but we don't have his home address on file. The file has a note that he will supply an address later. However, we do have his cell phone number."

The manager looked at Jeannie and Max and asked, "Do you want me to contact James Rivas using his cell phone number? It might help us gather more information about the cab and the incident in question."

"No, not yet," Jeannie said to the manager. She continued, "When you summon Rivas for a driving assignment, how long does it typically take for him to respond?"

"Usually about half an hour, not more," the manager replied. Jeannie glanced at Max and signaled for him to step away from the manager.

"Call for backup. We require a minimum of five officers dressed in plain clothes and driving unmarked cars to be strategically positioned around the business. Once they are in place, I will instruct the manager to contact Rivas."

Jeannie excused herself from the manager and informed him that if he wished to resume his regular duties, she would find him when she needed him to make the call. She emphasized the importance of keeping their conversation confidential.

29

CHAPTER

At 11:15 a.m., Jeannie and her team of officers stood prepared. She directed the manager to contact Rivas and request his presence at the office, emphasizing the need for him to bring his logbook. The manager assured Jeannie that the message would be delivered in a nonchalant manner, as occasional requests of this nature were a routine part of the job, and drivers willingly complied to maintain their employment status.

Jeannie was provided with a detailed description of Rivas's usual truck—a black 2004 Dodge Rumble Bee pickup—making it easily recognizable for her undercover officers. At 12:10 p.m., Jeannie received confirmation that Rivas had just arrived and turned into the parking lot. Observing him in a relaxed manner, he strolled towards the main entrance, holding his logbook, and headed for the manager's office. Jeannie and Max were already concealed inside, positioned near the door.

Rivas knocked on the door, and upon the manager's invitation, he entered the office. As he stepped inside, Max discreetly closed the door behind him. The manager excused himself from the room, leaving Jeannie and Max alone with Rivas. Jeannie extended her badge, promptly identifying herself and Max as law enforcement officers. They requested Rivas to take a seat, signaling that they needed to speak with him.

"Can you tell me what this is all about?" Rivas asked, curiosity evident in his voice.

"Can I see your logbook?" Max responded, bypassing Rivas's question. Rivas obliged and handed over his logbook. Jeannie maintained her silence as Max flipped through the pages, carefully examining the entries. After a moment, Max glanced at Jeannie and nodded, signaling that something significant had been found.

"Your name is James Rivas. Is that correct?" Jeannie inquired, breaking her silence.

"Yes," Rivas confirmed.

"When was your last drive for the company?" Jeannie continued her line of questioning.

"I finished up late last night when I dropped my rig off. That's it out there," Rivas pointed toward his cab.

Jeannie opened her binder, revealing a photograph of their most recent victim. "Have you ever seen this girl?" she asked, presenting the picture to Rivas. Rivas quickly glanced at the image and denied ever having seen her before. Jeannie pressed further, "Where did you last fuel up?"

"Oh, hell, let me think. Can I look at my logbook?" Rivas requested, attempting to buy himself some time to cover his tracks. Both Jeannie and Max were aware he was stalling. Max handed Rivas his logbook, and Rivas immediately found his entry for refueling, conveniently bypassing the stop where he had picked up the victim. Sensing his attempt to deceive, Rivas provided information that Jeannie and Max knew was a lie.

"Mr. Rivas, we have a problem," Jeannie stated, a sarcastic smile playing on her lips. "You see, here is a fuel receipt that bears your signature from this truck stop. Care to explain that?"

"Okay, you got me. I fudged my logbook, but every trucker does that. I admit, I was there," Rivas confessed, attempting to downplay the severity of his actions. He tried to employ his charm and good looks to maneuver himself out of the situation. "When did fudging on logbooks become a federal crime investigated by the FBI?"

"We don't investigate falsifying logbook entries, Mr. Rivas," Jeannie responded, her tone firm. "But we do investigate kidnappings and homicides that occur across state lines."

Rivas's demeanor swiftly changed. He started to rise from his seat but was firmly instructed by Max to remain seated. "This is a bunch of bullshit. This is entrapment. You called me in here under false pretenses, and now you're violating my rights," Rivas protested.

Jeannie leaned forward, her face inches away from Rivas'. "No, Mr. Rivas, we have not violated your rights. However, at this moment, I will read you your rights," she declared sternly. With a scowl on his face and a look of hatred, Rivas begrudgingly sat as Jeannie recited his Miranda Rights.

After finishing, Jeannie asked Rivas if he understood his rights. "Fuck you, bitch. You think you're something special, don't you? Blond hair, blue eyes, nice ass," he sneered, directing his venomous words at Jeannie. "You don't have any evidence. What do you have, a picture of me talking to some slut? Yeah, so what? I pick up a lot of hitchhikers. You think you're better than me? I wish I would have picked you up on the interstate. Fuck you, and you too," he added, glancing at Max. "I want an attorney right now."

"Well, Mr. Rivas, this is what is going to happen," Jeannie calmly responded, undeterred by Rivas's hostile outburst. "We will obtain a search warrant for that cab over there, which you admitted you drove and dropped off last night. I assume your fingerprints will be all over the inside."

"That's what I said, bitch. You've got nothing. I'm going to sue both of you and the fucking FBI," Rivas retorted, confidence dripping from his words.

"Please, Mr. Rivas, let me finish," Jeannie said with a composed smile, maintaining her professionalism. Rivas simply glared at her, seething with anger. "Now, our forensic team is one of the best in the country. I know you believe you're in the clear when it comes to evidence left behind by the victim, as the company cleans and washes the entire cab after each run. However, you would be amazed at what our technicians can find. All it takes is a partial fingerprint, maybe some semen stains or strands of hair, for our experts to uncover. Oh, and I almost forgot—we will be searching both your truck and your residence."

The mention of a thorough forensic investigation seemed to rattle Rivas, momentarily cracking his defiant facade. Jeannie motioned to Max to cuff Rivas. Rivas tried to rush to the door, but Jeannie punched him squarely in the stomach, causing him to bend over and gasp for air. "That's for the victims, you piece of shit." Max applied the cuffs behind Rivas' back and helped him straighten up. "Can you get him to the patrol car?" Jeannie asked. "Oh, and request forensic to respond ASAP."

"Not a problem," Max said. "I notified the other units that he was in custody, and they are waiting in the parking lot to get a look at him."

"Great. I'll meet you outside shortly," Jeannie replied. There was something she needed to take care of. Making sure no one was nearby, Jeannie opened the passenger door of the cab. She retrieved the folded plastic glove containing strands of blond hair she had taken from the victim earlier in the day and carefully rubbed them into the carpet fiber beneath the passenger side window. Satisfied with her work, she closed the door. To make it obvious that the cab was now part of a crime scene, she stretched police crime scene barricade tape across both doors and then went off looking for the manager.

One of the other officers from the task force approached Jeannie, offering assistance. Jeannie assigned him the task of watching over the cab until the forensics team arrived. Once they completed their evidence collection, the officer would return the cab to the manager, whom Jeannie had thanked for his cooperation.

30

CHAPTER

The briefing room buzzed with jubilation as the task force members congratulated one another. Jeannie had Max call a local bakery, which gladly agreed to provide several cakes at no charge to enhance the celebratory atmosphere. The Chief of Police enthusiastically offered handshakes to anyone who would accept, and while some reluctantly obliged, many reciprocated the gesture. It was only a matter of time before a swarm of media personnel would descend upon the other side of the substation, hungry for their share of the evening's events to feature on the evening news.

Jeannie delegated the task of disseminating information to the Chief, who relished being the center of attention. And why not, Jeannie thought. If he was contemplating retirement, what better way to conclude his career than by solving the case of a ruthless killer who had been terrorizing the community for an unknown time?

As the celebrations continued, Jeannie couldn't help but feel a sense of relief wash over her. She would have to stand by the Chief's side during the media frenzy, but her mind was already focused on one thing—returning to her cabin and finally getting a well-deserved rest in her own bed.

Amid the excitement, Max managed to navigate his way through the crowd of jubilant task force officers, many of whom were indulging in second and third helpings of cake. "Jeannie, good news!" Max exclaimed, his eyes gleaming with excitement. "The forensic team found several blond hairs in the truck's cab. Wanna bet they belong to our victim?"

A genuine smile crossed Jeannie's face. "From your lips to God's ears," she replied, grateful that forensics found the hair fibers. This concrete evidence linking the perpetrator to their victim would be hard for his defense to explain away. Of course, the asshole could also use an insanity defense, but either way, Rivas would be gone for a long, long time.

Jeannie set the slices of cake on the kitchen counter as she listened to Ismail's voice on the other end of the line. The news of her triumphant capture of the serial killer had quickly spread, and now Ismail was calling to share updates and seek her opinion.

"Hello, Ace," Jeannie greeted him. "Clean out my office? Boss lady is coming home."

Ismail chuckled. "Gee, here I was calling to congratulate you, and you're already throwing me out of my office. Typical."

Jeannie joined in the laughter, appreciating the lighthearted banter amid their serious work. "Well, you know how it is. Gotta make room for the boss." They exchanged a few more pleasantries before Ismail shifted the conversation to the details of his respective case. Jeannie listened attentively as Ismail shared his findings.

"That's the other reason I called," Ismail continued. "This asshole has been following a distinct pattern. He kills his victims every seven days, like clockwork. But then, three days later, he goes after a Hispanic male. Have you ever heard of a serial killer changing his modus operandi so drastically?"

Jeannie furrowed her brow, contemplating the significance of Ismail's observation. The unexpected deviation from the established pattern raised intriguing questions. "No, it's unusual," she replied thoughtfully. "Most serial killers tend to stick to their signature patterns. It could indicate a shift in motive or some external influence. We'll have to dig deeper and see if there's a connection between his victims and the change in his pattern."

"That's the other reason I called. We found the connection. Our victims sat on the same jury. It was a molestation case and lasted two weeks. Darcy and Susan are checking the court records and jury lists, but my gut tells me this is the connection we have been looking for."

The wheels in Jeannie's mind began turning as she considered the possibilities, fully aware that their work was far from over. "That's fantastic," Jeannie exclaimed, her excitement evident in her voice. "Make sure everyone involved keeps this information strictly confidential. We can't afford to tip off the suspect."

"I'm going to call the Chief and inform him that it's crucial for me to hand over the case to the State Police and return to the bureau," Jeannie said, determination evident in her tone. She realized that their next steps would involve coordinating with different agencies to tie the suspects to their respective cases using the DNA evidence they had obtained. It was a matter of connecting the dots and bringing justice to all the victims.

"I'm planning to head back early tomorrow morning. I'll be sure to reach out to you on my way back, and we can discuss the next steps. Thanks for the great work, Ace." With a sense of accomplishment and anticipation for the work that lay ahead, Jeannie ended the call, ready to prepare for her journey back and the challenges that awaited her upon her return.

Upon arriving at the bureau, Darcy and Susan met him at the entrance door. Ismail listened intently as the two briefed him on the wealth of information they had gathered. The frustration he had felt earlier began to dissipate as he realized the progress they had made. He knew that Darcy and Susan were skilled investigators, and their findings could be crucial in cracking the case.

As they walked to the breakroom, Ismail's mind started racing with possibilities. He couldn't wait to go through the material and connect the dots. The thought of finally bringing closure to the case gave him renewed energy and determination.

Inside the breakroom, Ismail poured himself a cup of coffee while Darcy and Susan spread out the collected information on the table. The room buzzed with excitement as they began discussing their findings in detail. Ismail was impressed by the thoroughness of their research.

"Our victims sat on a jury where the accused, a Chris Grayson, was accused of molesting the young son of their next-door neighbor. Initially, it appears the suspect was afforded all of his rights and was dutifully convicted and sent to Folsom Prison. However, Grayson only lasted two months before he was stabbed to death by other inmates."

"Well, there is a hierarchy even in prison, and child molesters are at the bottom," Ismail said. "So where is the connection between the jury and the defendant?"

Ismail's mind raced as he processed the new information Susan had just shared. The connection between the jury and the defendant was a crucial piece of the puzzle that they had been missing. It seemed that the events surrounding Chris Grayson's conviction and subsequent death in prison were not as straightforward as they initially appeared.

It suggested a possible motive for someone seeking revenge for Grayson. However, it also raised questions about the integrity of the trial and whether there had been any foul play involved. Ismail turned to Susan and Darcy, a mix of concern and determination in his eyes. "We need to dig deeper into this connection," he said firmly. "We have to find out if there was any misconduct during the trial or if there's more to this story than meets the eye. This information could potentially unravel everything we thought we knew about this case."

Susan nodded in agreement, her expression mirroring Ismail's determination. "I'll start looking into the trial proceedings, a list of all the jurors, and the jurors' backgrounds," she said.

Darcy chimed in, her voice filled with resolve, "I'll focus on tracking down any leads related to Grayson's time in prison. Who visited him? If there were inmates who orchestrated his murder on behalf of someone outside. This might be linked to a larger criminal network. We need to find out who they were and if they had any ties to the victims or anyone involved in the trial."

"First and foremost, I need the list of the jurors and alternate jurors so we can contact them and alert the law enforcement agencies where they reside to be on the lookout for our killer. Also, and I know you both are extremely busy, but we need to find out everything we can about Grayson. His family, friends, co-workers; I mean everything. Let's gather the rest of the team and bring them up to speed," he said. "We'll assign specific tasks and coordinate our efforts to ensure we cover all angles. Time is of the essence, and we can't afford to overlook anything."

31

CHAPTER

As Jeannie drove, her mind wrestled with the two complex cases she was involved in. The Snow Angel investigation had consumed her thoughts for weeks, but now, the news of Ismail's breakthrough in the case brought a glimmer of hope in the Numbers Killings. She knew it was crucial to keep the momentum going.

She had to push the Snow Angel case into the recesses of her brain. The pattern of the Numbers Killings haunted her, especially now that the killings were coming quicker. She couldn't shake the sense of urgency to uncover the perpetrator's identity. Jeannie knew that focusing on one case at a time was necessary to maintain clarity, but the lines between the two investigations blurred in her mind.

Despite the temptation to call Jessie and share the news about Ismail's progress, Jeannie decided against it. She yearned to get home, take a hot shower, and have a moment of respite before the demanding day that awaited her at the bureau. Time was of the essence, and every minute counted.

She reminded herself that she would have the opportunity to discuss the breakthrough with Jessie and the rest of the team once she returned to the bureau. They could strategize and determine the best course of action together. Right now, her priority was to rejuvenate herself and prepare for the long day ahead.

As she pulled into her driveway, Jeannie made a mental note to set her alarm a little earlier than usual. There was no time to waste. A hot shower, a quick rest, and a renewed mindset were all she needed.

"Well, we made the news again," Adam said. They are calling it the 'Numbers Killings.' Not bad for a name, I guess."

"I got an email from you know who. He said the police are a little baffled by us taking out that gay dude three days after our last. They were hoping that the seven days between incidents was going to lead to a pattern," Ariana replied. "I wonder when we'll get the information on our next target?"

"Hey, maybe we can do two in one day," Adam said excitedly.

Jeannie arrived early the next morning, opting for two frozen pieces of French toast that she popped into the toaster. After finishing, she fed her koi in the dining room and her outside pond. With a steel coffee tumbler in hand, she hopped into her sports car and headed for the Dumbarton Bridge.

As Jeannie drove towards the bureau, she let the wind from the bay blow through her hair, enjoying the refreshing feeling. Once she arrived, as usual, she would put her hair in a ponytail. Despite the previous day's activities and the long drive from Idaho, Jeannie had managed to sleep soundly.

The combination of physical exhaustion and the satisfaction of capturing a long-awaited suspect had brought her much-needed rest. Now, however, she had to shift her focus and assist Ismail and his team in putting an end to the Numbers investigation.

As Jeannie entered the bureau, she was relieved to see that only a few agents were present, just as she had hoped. The quiet atmosphere gave her the opportunity to focus on her tasks without being immediately bombarded with accolades and congratulations for the successful conclusion of the Snow Angel investigation.

Making her way to her office, Jeannie settled in and began sorting through her phone messages and the items in her inbox. She knew that there would be important messages to attend to and updates to review, requiring her undivided attention. Taking this moment to herself allowed her to gather her thoughts and prioritize her responsibilities for the day ahead.

With her phone messages and inbox in order, Jeannie felt more prepared and organized to tackle the challenges that awaited her. She was ready to face the day and provide the necessary support to her colleagues in the ongoing Numbers investigation. Feeling the need for a coffee refill, Jeannie grabbed her cup and made her way to the break room. As she filled her cup, the sound of more agents arriving and the buzz of conversation filled the air, indicating that the office was getting busier.

With her freshly filled coffee cup in hand, Jeannie prepared herself to 'face the music,' knowing that the accolades and inquiries about the Snow Angel investigation would soon come pouring in. She braced herself for the inevitable wave of attention and discussions that would surround her successful accomplishment.

Taking a deep breath, Jeannie stepped out of the break room, ready to engage with her fellow agents and face the day head-on. She understood the importance of teamwork and camaraderie within the bureau, and she was prepared to contribute her expertise and support to her colleagues as they worked on the Numbers investigation together.

As the SAC, Special Agent in Charge Lomax, arrived at the bureau, he immediately sought out Jeannie. With a warm smile, he shook her hand, acknowledging the impressive job she had done.

"That was one hell of a job you did," he praised her. "I'm proud of you. They will be talking about this case in the BAU for sure." His words reflected the significance of Jeannie's accomplishment and the impact it would have on her professional reputation.

SAC Lomax then expressed his concern for her well-being, questioning if she should be present at the bureau. He mentioned Idaho and suggested that Jeannie might need a few days off to wrap things up there. He recognized her hard work and believed she deserved some time to rest and recover from the intense investigation.

Jeannie appreciated the SAC's kind words and concern. She knew she had pushed herself to the limit in solving the Snow Angel case, but she also understood the importance of her role in the ongoing Numbers investigation. She replied respectfully, "Thank you. I appreciate your support and recognition. I feel rested, and I believe it's crucial for me to be here to contribute to the Numbers investigation, especially with the killer reducing the number of days between incidents. Once we make progress on that front, I'll take some time off to ensure everything is wrapped up in Idaho. I want to see this case through, sir."

Jeannie's dedication to her work was evident, and SAC Lomax nodded, acknowledging her commitment. "I understand," he said. "Just remember to take care of yourself, and don't hesitate to reach out if you need anything."

"Well, it's about time you left God's country and came back to earn your paycheck," a smiling Ismail said as he snuck up behind Jeannie and waited for Lomax to leave. He then bowed twice for effect.

"Aw, you did miss me?" Jeannie replied. "Did you clean out my office?" she asked jokingly.

"Yes, I cleaned my stuff out. With you leaving all the time due to your fame, I think I should move my desk into your office. What do you think?"

"Fat chance. Besides, Lomax was just talking about recommending you for that Fairbanks, Alaska SAC job."

"Yeah, yeah. You up for another cup of coffee, and I can bring you up to speed?" he asked as they headed for the breakroom.

32

CHAPTER

The large briefing room buzzed with activity as Ismail's team settled down. Jeannie, respecting Ismail's leadership in the investigation, took a seat in the front row. She understood the importance of allowing Ismail to lead the briefing and set the tone for the meeting.

As the team members gathered, Jeannie observed their focused expressions and felt a sense of determination in the room. Each person had played a crucial role so far in the Numbers investigation, and now they were ready to share their findings, discuss strategies, and collaborate on the next steps.

Ismail, standing at the front of the room, exuded a calm confidence. He greeted his team with a nod and began the briefing, outlining the progress they had made thus far and highlighting key pieces of evidence they had gathered.

As Ismail began the briefing, he acknowledged Jeannie's presence and her recent success in solving the Snow Angel case in Idaho. The room erupted in applause, filled with admiration and respect for Jeannie's achievements.

Feeling a blush creeping up her cheeks, Jeannie decided to remain seated and simply wave her hand in acknowledgment. She appreciated the support and recognition from her colleagues but preferred to maintain a humble demeanor.

As the applause subsided, Ismail continued with the briefing, smoothly transitioning into an overview of the current progress in the Numbers investigation. Jeannie's focus shifted back to the task at hand, eager to contribute her insights and expertise to the ongoing case.

Jeannie listened attentively, her mind analyzing the information presented. She admired Ismail's ability to effectively communicate complex details, engaging the team and fostering a sense of unity among them. Jeannie then noticed that Darcy wasn't present. She knew that Ismail had assigned another agent to work with Darcy, but for the life of her, she couldn't remember her name. She turned her attention back to the briefing.

Almost on cue, Ismail turned the team's attention to the progress made by Darcy and Susan Richards in their records search. Jeannie leaned forward, her anticipation growing. She sensed that the information they had uncovered could potentially hold the key to identifying the elusive killer in the numbers investigation.

Everyone's attention turned to the entrance of both agents, who rushed into the room and upfront next to Ismail. Ismail asked Jeannie to join them. "You won't believe what we found," Susan said excitedly. "The case was very weak, but the defendant had a lengthy rap sheet which did not go in his favor. Anyway, the whole case hinged on the testimony of not just the young molestation victim but also of her father, who had a hatred for the defendant. He was convicted and, as you know, later killed in prison."

Darcy then revealed the most intriguing finding—the defendant's genealogy. "He had a wife named Theresa Grayson and two children, Ariana and Adam. The siblings had a history of delinquency, involving crimes including burglary, car theft, robbery, and even cruelty to animals."

Ismail wasted no time in asking about the whereabouts of Mrs. Grayson and the two children. Susan responded, informing them that Mrs. Grayson had tragically taken her own life upon learning about her husband's death. As for Ariana and Adam, they were no longer children. Ariana was in her late twenties, while Adam had recently turned twenty-two. The team was currently working on tracking down their current location.

Jeannie's mind raced with the implications of this new information. The connection between the defendant and the two children raised intriguing possibilities. Could Ariana and Adam be involved in the Numbers killings? Were they seeking revenge for their father's conviction and subsequent death? These questions needed answers. She could see in Ismail's face that he was thinking the same thing.

As the team absorbed the news, Ismail emphasized the importance of tracking down Ariana and Adam. He recognized that they could hold valuable information that would help advance the investigation and bring them closer to apprehending the true culprit behind the Numbers Killings.

"Wait, there's more," Susan said, looking at her stack of papers. "The defendant, Mr. Grayson, had a previous marriage which resulted in one child, a son."

"So that makes him Ariana and Adam's step-brother," Jeannie interjected.

"His name is Jessie Thompson." As Susan revealed the name of the older step-brother, Jeannie's stomach filled with acid, and a sense of unease washed over her. She felt like she was about to vomit. She instinctively braced herself, gripping the table that held the documents laid out by Susan and Darcy.

Ismail, recognizing the gravity of the situation, swiftly made a decision. He instructed the assembled group of agents to take a fifteen-minute break, allowing them time to process the new information.

Meanwhile, he, Jeannie, Darcy, and Susan left the room, heading towards Darcy's office.

Jeannie's mind raced with a mix of emotions. The connection between Jessie Thompson and the ongoing investigation was undeniable, and it brought forth a wave of concern and apprehension. She knew that delving deeper into Jessie's background and her personal involvement with him would preclude her from actively participating any further in the investigation.

As they entered Darcy's office, the atmosphere became more intense. "Sorry, Jeannie," a sincere Ismail stated. Darcy and Susan did not understand Ismail's comment. Jeannie took a seat, her mind still reeling from the revelations.

Jeannie looked at Darcy and Susan. As Jeannie revealed the startling truth about Jessie Thompson, the team was taken aback by the unexpected connection since only Ismail knew of the budding relationship between the two. Darcy and Susan expressed their sympathy, realizing the uncomfortable position Jeannie found herself in due to her previous involvement with him.

Darcy embraced Jeannie, offering her comfort and support amid this development. The weight of the situation hung heavy in the room, and the team understood the need to act swiftly and decisively.

Jeannie turned her attention to Ismail, knowing that Jessie Thompson's involvement would have significant implications for the investigation. She suggested that Ismail call for the SAC to come down to Darcy's office, as a discussion about their next course of action was imperative. Recognizing the importance of involving the SAC in this critical development, Ismail swiftly left the office, heading towards Lomax's office to convey the urgency of the situation.

Jeannie understood that her role in the investigation would likely be limited moving forward, as directed by the SAC. The revelation of her past connection with Jessie Thompson added an additional layer of complexity to the case, requiring careful consideration of the team's approach.

Jeannie's emotions swirled within her as she waited for the SAC to arrive. Discomfort and regret washed over her, knowing that her personal connection with Jessie Thompson had unintentionally intertwined her life with the ongoing investigation. However, these emotions fueled her determination to ensure justice was served, regardless of the personal implications.

Jeannie firmly believed that Jessie Thompson's involvement in the Numbers Killings needed to be addressed, and if the evidence pointed in that direction, his arrest would be an imperative step.

As the door to the office opened, indicating the SAC's arrival, Jeannie took a deep breath, steadying herself. She knew the forthcoming discussion would require careful navigation and clear communication of the facts at hand. The SAC looked concerned, but at the same time, a sense of calmness arrived with him.

"So, we have a slight problem with the possibility that instead of a lone killer, we may actually have a team of three involved with the murders," Lomax said before sitting in a chair.

No one was sure who should respond first, but Jeannie replied, "Ismail and I met with the head of the SFPD homicide division, where we were introduced to the lead investigator of what the media is now calling the 'Numbers Killings.' At that time, there was a mutual interest between Sergeant Jessie Thompson and me that led to a dinner date a few days later." She looked Lomax in the eyes. "It never went beyond dinner since the next morning I drove to Idaho." She paused, holding back tears.

Acknowledging Jeannie's concern, the SAC assured her that she could continue working with Ismail on the case but strictly from the confines of the bureau. He emphasized the need for caution, stressing that Jeannie should steer clear of crime scenes and other potentially compromising situations. The objective was to maintain the integrity of the investigation while minimizing any potential vulnerabilities in court.

The SAC took responsibility for initiating legal procedures to obtain a wiretap on Thompson's cell phone, recognizing its potential value in gathering crucial evidence. He assured Jeannie that he would also coordinate with Thompson's chief, ensuring that the necessary information remained confidential to avoid tipping off the suspect or suspects.

Jeannie felt a sense of calmness wash over her as the SAC conveyed his trust in her abilities and provided guidance for the next steps. She understood the importance of following protocol and the need to maintain a professional distance from the case despite her personal connection with Thompson.

CHAPTER 33

Ismail asked Darcy and Susan to give him the room with Jeannie. As they shut the door behind them, Ismail walked up to Jeannie and put his hand on her shoulder. "You, okay?" he asked sincerely.

"I feel so stupid. How could I have fallen for that asshole?" Jeannie said, starting to cry.

"Hey, he's a nice-looking guy. Not as handsome as me, but I could see how a female might be attracted to him." Jeannie laughed as she wiped her eyes with a Kleenex. She got off Darcy's desk.

Ismail's genuine concern and attempt to lighten the mood with a touch of humor brought a momentary smile to Jeannie's face amid her tears. She appreciated his support and the reminder to approach the situation with caution.

"You're right. We can't jump to conclusions just yet," Jeannie replied, her voice still tinged with vulnerability. "But the evidence and connections we've uncovered so far are troubling. I can't help but feel a sense of betrayal and disappointment."

Ismail nodded, understanding the emotional turmoil Jeannie was experiencing. "It's natural to feel that way. We still aren't 100% sure of any of the three's involvement. We trusted him, and it hurts to discover that he may be involved in these murders. But we have to follow the evidence and see where it leads us."

Jeannie took a deep breath, regained some composure, and stood. "You're right. We can't let personal emotions cloud our judgment." She gave Ismail a long, warm hug.

"Hey, now don't go all Hallmark on me. We need to focus on the investigation, gather more evidence, and build a solid case, and if Thompson is involved, we'll put his sorry ass in jail. You heard Lomax. You need to steer clear of crime scenes and other potentially compromising situations, but I have an idea. Does he know you are back from Idaho yet?"

"No. As far as he knows, I'm still up in Idaho. Why?" Jeannie asked.

A few hours later, Ismail had received word that Lomax had secured a search warrant for Thompson's cell and work phones. Both were now wiretapped and being monitored by Burk. Jeannie and Ismail entered the soundproof room where Burk was set up.

Jeannie checked to see if he and Burk were ready. Both put their earphones on as Jeannie placed the call.

"Jeannie, you're back! Congratulations. Wow. What a feather in your cap. Your investigation ranks right up there with the Green River Killer murder investigation. When did you get in?" Thompson asked. Jeannie could hear officers talking in the background, so she assumed he was in the homicide division.

"Thank you, Jessie," Jeannie replied, a sense of pride evident in her voice while disguising her contempt for him. "I just got in a couple of hours ago. It's been an intense and challenging investigation, but we finally got a break. I can't share all the details over the phone."

"No, of course not. I understand. As soon as you rest up, let me know, and perhaps we can take in a movie and dinner," Thompson asked with a little flirtation in his voice.

"That sounds good." As Jeannie spoke, she glanced at Ismail while giving her cell phone the finger. She continued the conversation, keeping her tone casual but alert. "How's everything at the homicide division? I can hear the buzz in the background. Any interesting cases going on?"

Thompson's voice sounded a bit distant as he responded, likely preoccupied with the ongoing activities. "Yeah, it's been pretty busy lately. We've got a couple of high-profile cases on our hands, including a cold case that's resurfaced. But I have to say, your investigation has really stolen the spotlight. You've made quite a name for yourself, Jeannie. By the way, have you talked with Ismail? I'm wondering how his serial case is going. I haven't talked to him recently."

Jeannie winked at Ismail. "Well, I just got off the phone with him. He's following up a hot lead, a major break in the case, he feels."

"Really?" a concerned Thompson replied. "What kind of breakthrough?"

"I don't know; I was so tired that I told him good luck and that I would see him in the morning. If I hear anything tomorrow, I will let you know."

"Okay," Thompson said with disappointment in his voice. "I'll talk to you tomorrow. Get some rest." He abruptly hung up. Jeannie and Ismail exchanged a knowing look as Jeannie ended her call with Thompson. The plan was unfolding smoothly, and she was playing her part convincingly.

"Wait for it," Ismail said in anticipation that his cell phone would ring. Sure enough, Thompson was calling him.

"Flores," Ismail said after answering acting as if he were out of breath.

"Ismail, it's Jessie Thompson. I thought I'd check in and see how your investigation is going."

"Oh, we just got a huge break. I'm working with my IT people to track down some promising leads. I really can't talk now. Things are moving pretty fast. I'll call you later."

"Nice job, Ismail," Jeannie whispered a hint of excitement in her voice. "Thompson bought it. Now that we've successfully created the illusion of a major breakthrough, let's focus on our next move."

Ismail nodded. "Okay, Burkman, this is now in your ballpark. Find out who Thompson calls." Ismail's eyes gleamed with anticipation.

"Ismail, gather the team," Jeannie instructed, her voice steady. "We need to get ready to mobilize. Burk will share the phone number of Thompson's call, and then Darcy can locate Adam's, Ariana's, or both addresses.

As Ismail left to assemble the team, Jeannie took a deep breath, a mix of nerves and excitement coursing through her veins. They were closing in on the suspects. This was the pivotal moment in the investigation, and they had to make it count. The phone call had served its purpose, but now it was time for real progress.

34

CHAPTER

Darcy and Susan walked briskly down to Jeannie's office. Not finding her there, they headed to the briefing room where Ismail and Jeannie were discussing the progress in the case as well as issuing assignments at whatever location the call from Thompson was received.

Seeing the two agents, Ismail asked, "Did you get it?"

"Yes," Darcy said. "You won't believe it, but it went to a home phone rather than a cell in the Tenderloin area here in the city. Here's the address." Jeannie and Ismail looked at it.

"Here," Jeannie said, turning her laptop over to Darcy. "Do a Google search and project an overhead shot of the residence and neighbors." Darcy quickly did so, and soon, everyone in the room saw the address of interest.

As Darcy projected the overhead shot of the residence and its surroundings onto the screen, Jeannie and Ismail examined the image closely. The neighborhood appeared to be a rundown area, fitting the Tenderloin district's profile.

Jeannie's eyes narrowed as she studied the image. "This is it," she said with a mix of determination and anticipation. "Our breakthrough has led us straight to the heart of the investigation. This residence might hold the key to uncovering the truth."

Susan, who had been silently observing, spoke up. "We should move quickly and secure the location. We don't want to give anyone the chance to cover their tracks or destroy evidence."

Ismail nodded in agreement. "Agreed. I'll order the tactical team to get ready. We need to approach this with caution and precision."

Darcy, already prepared for this moment, quickly got on the phone, calling in additional units and requesting backup from the appropriate departments. The urgency in her voice reflected the gravity of the situation.

Jeannie, meanwhile, pulled up relevant information about the residence on her computer. She scanned through any available records, looking for any clues or connections that could aid their operation.

Darcy and Susan immediately began distributing pictures of Ariana and Adam to all the officers.

Each team member would be equipped with visual references to ensure accurate identification and prevent any potential mistakes.

Jeannie's voice resonated with a mix of determination and caution. "Remember, our primary goal is to apprehend Ariana and Adam safely, but we must prioritize the safety of innocent civilians and ourselves. Be prepared for any scenario and act accordingly." The team members nodded in understanding as Jeannie conveyed the gravity of the situation. The stakes were high, and they were prepared for the potential dangers they might face.

She continued, emphasizing the importance of precision and coordination. "The tactical team will approach the residence strategically, maintaining communication and visual contact at all times. Just in case the suspects escape our net, that is where you all come in. Be alert for these two trying to leave the area."

Jeannie's gaze met each team member's eyes, ensuring they were all present and focused. "Stay sharp, stay vigilant. We're here to bring justice and protect our community. Let's go out there and make a difference."

With those final words, the team members prepared themselves physically and mentally. They checked their equipment, adjusted their gear, and double-checked their communication devices. Each member understood the importance of their role in the upcoming operation.

"Everyone, gear up and stay focused," Jeannie said firmly. "Your primary job is to take up positions here, here, and here." She then turned to the assembled officers. "Probably don't need to tell you, but one of these two, or perhaps both, have already killed five innocent people. They are probably not going to surrender."

"He sounded kind of freaked out today," Ariana said to her brother, not expecting a reply. "At least we have the name and picture of our next target. This is the first time he told us to expedite. I mean, I was just kidding the other day suggesting that we take two people out on the same day."

She turned her gaze to Adam, who was cleaning the .22 revolver. "Well, he just realizes that with the FBI involved and with seven more jurors, the prosecutor, and the judge left to be eliminated, we need to move faster," Adam said calmly. "We can go out tonight and check on the first of the next two and at least see where the other one lives. Then, we take them out on the same day."

"Unit one, are you in position?" Ismail asked.

"Roger that," came the response.

"Unit two?" he asked next.

"In position," the agent responded. Satisfied that the two main intersections were being monitored, Ismail gave the tactical team the green light. They sprang into action, following their carefully planned approach. Now, he and Jeannie waited anxiously. Time seemed to stretch as Ismail and Jeannie exchanged glances, their unspoken words conveying their shared anticipation and determination. They knew the risks involved, but their commitment to justice drove them forward.

Finally, the crackle of the radio broke the silence. "Tactical one, visual contact confirmed," came the voice over the transmission. "Ariana and Adam are inside the residence."

A surge of adrenaline coursed through Ismail and Jeannie's' veins. The moment they had been waiting for had arrived. They maintained their positions, their hearts pounding with a mixture of tension and hope as they focused on their radios.

The sound of gunshots pierced the air, shattering the tension and plunging the scene into chaos. Ismail and Jeannie's instincts kicked in as they registered the distinct sounds of different firearms being discharged.

Jeannie's eyes widened, her earlier assessment ringing true. The suspects were indeed prepared for a fight and showed no intention of surrendering peacefully.

As the chaos subsided, a heavy silence settled over the scene. The echoes of gunfire were replaced by a stillness that hung in the air as the weight of the moment sank in. Ismail and Jeannie exchanged glances, their eyes reflecting a mix of relief and somberness.

The tactical commander's voice broke through the tense quiet over the radio, delivering the sobering confirmation of the outcome. "Code four. Two down, deceased." Two lives had been lost, bringing an end to the threat posed by Ariana and Adam.

Ismail, maintaining his composure, acknowledged the report on the radio. "Copy that. Secure the scene and ensure the safety of all personnel," he responded, his voice carrying a tone of solemnity.

Together, Ismail and Jeannie approached the scene, their eyes scanning the area. The gravity of the moment was palpable as they assessed the aftermath of the intense encounter. As the team worked to secure the area and begin the necessary investigative procedures, Ismail and Jeannie shared a mutual understanding.

When they entered the rundown residence, they saw Ariana lying on the floor on her side next to a rifle. Sitting on the couch, with a .22 revolver near his right hand, sat Adam, his shirt filling with blood that was spilling out on the couch. Several entrance wounds could be seen.

Both Jeannie and Ismail knew that the investigation was far from over, as they would need to thoroughly examine the scene, gather evidence, and ensure a comprehensive understanding of the events that had unfolded. And there was the matter of Jessie Thompson.

Jeannie assigned several officers to the crime scene and notified the coroner's office and the shooting review team for those officers who fired the shots from the tactical team. After notifying Lomax of the outcome, Jeannie and Ismail headed to the San Francisco Police Department.

CHAPTER 35

The sudden and shocking turn of events unfolded with rapid intensity. Jeannie, still seated in the car, froze momentarily as the sound of a gunshot reached her ears. Her heart sank, realizing the gravity of the situation. Without hesitation, she swiftly exited the vehicle and rushed towards the homicide division, her mind racing with concern for Ismail's safety and the well-being of her colleagues. She knew that time was of the essence and that she needed to assess the situation.

As Jeannie entered the room, the atmosphere was heavy with shock and confusion. Thompson lay motionless on the ground, the aftermath of his desperate act evident. The detectives who had taken cover slowly began to rise, their expressions a mix of disbelief and sorrow.

Ismail, his voice filled with urgency, called for medical assistance over the radio. The gravity of the situation weighed heavily upon him, as he had been unable to prevent Thompson from taking such drastic action.

Jeannie, overcome with a mixture of emotions, approached Ismail. Her concern for him and the toll this ordeal had taken on their team was evident in her eyes. She spoke with a combination of determination and empathy. "Ismail, are you okay?" He did not reply but nodded his head.

The other agents in the room, still processing the shocking turn of events, slowly regained their composure. They joined Jeannie and Ismail, ready to provide any necessary assistance and support in the aftermath of the tragedy. The homicide division now became a crime scene.

As they awaited the coroner's arrival, Lomax entered. He quietly looked over at Jeannie and Ismail and the body of Thompson. Together, all three would find the strength to move forward, even in the face of the unexpected and devastating events of the day.

Ismail told Lomax about how the event went down with enough information so the SAC could fill the coroner in when she arrived.

"This place is going to be crawling with media soon. I want the two of you to return to the bureau. The Chief and I will hold a short press conference here to feed the vultures. We'll give them enough to satisfy their new stations for today. We'll do a follow-up press conference tomorrow after you two get a good night's sleep. Now, get the hell out of here," a smiling Lomax said.

Jeannie and Ismail nodded, appreciating Lomax's understanding and support in such a difficult situation. They understood the importance of managing the media.

Jeannie's pleasant afternoon by the koi pond was interrupted by the unexpected call from Max Elders. While she hoped for a moment of respite, she couldn't help but anticipate that the nature of the call might involve another grim investigation.

As she answered the phone, her cheerful yet stern tone conveyed a mix of curiosity and a touch of caution. Jeannie had grown accustomed to the unpredictable nature of her work, but she was also eager to enjoy a well-deserved break.

"Max, don't you dare tell me you have another murder on your hands," she said, her voice carrying a hint of playfulness while still conveying her determination. She awaited Max's response, preparing herself for any news he might have to share. The tranquility of her surroundings contrasted with the potential darkness that awaited on the other end of the line.

"Hi, Jeannie. No. No more murders so far. But I thought you would like to know that they just took a person of interest into custody for the college student massacre. It's on television right now."

Jeannie got up and beelined it into her house to turn on her television. "Tell me what you know," she said to Max, somewhat out of breath from her walk from the outside. Jeannie's heart raced as she absorbed Max's update on the developments in the college student massacre case. The information he shared piqued her interest and ignited her investigative instincts.

She quickly turned her attention to the television to get the latest coverage. The gravity of the situation weighed heavily on her as she awaited further details from Max.

Listening intently, she learned that the suspect was a Ph.D. student in criminology at a nearby college. The coincidence struck her as fascinating and potentially significant. The connection between the suspect's field of study and the nature of the crime raised questions that demanded answers.

Jeannie's mind raced, contemplating the possibilities and implications of this new development. The potential motive, the suspect's knowledge of criminal behavior, and the connection to the victims all seemed to converge in an intriguing manner. Then, she caught herself. It was not her case. As she reminded herself of this fact, she continued to listen to both Max and Newsmax on the television.

"Well, I don't know all the particulars, but I know they found a blood-stained sheath at the crime scene on the bed near one of the victims when the murders were reported. It had blood from the victims but also from an unknown person." The subsequent use of genealogy search tools to identify a suspect intrigued her.

"The investigators use a genealogy search, you know, like Ancestry.com, FamilySearch, etc., one of those," Max continued, "And they got a hit."

Elders paused, realizing Jeannie was processing what she had said when he and his partner had contacted her at her cabin. "The guy is a loner. While the investigators were connecting the dots, they followed him from where he lives, which is pretty close to the crime scene, all the way back to his parents' house in Pennsylvania. They had him under surveillance, and when he dumped his trash …"

"They gathered it up and made a comparison resulting in his arrest," Jeannie said, finishing up for Elders.

"Bingo. And I have something else to share. Rivas is no longer among the living."

"What? What happened?" Jeannie quickly asked.

"He complained all the way through his trial that he was framed and that someone planted evidence in his truck." Max laughed while Jeannie smiled.

"Well, once it got out that he had killed so many young girls, some of the inmates took matters into their own hands while he was showering. Sure saved the taxpayers a ton of money."

"I'll be damned. I'm sure some of the victim's families would agree with you."

CHAPTER 36

As Jeannie arrived at Ismail's house, she noticed the lively atmosphere filled with the aroma of barbecue and the sound of laughter. His children were splashing in their inground pool, screaming at Jeannie to hurry up and join them. Ismail greeted Jeannie with a warm smile and a hug. He was wearing his red swim trunks and red, white, and blue tank top, covered by an apron stating something to the effect that he was the world's greatest BBQer.

"I'm so glad you're here, boss!" Ismail exclaimed. "We've got a lot of delicious food prepared by yours truly. I can't wait for you to try my grilled specialties."

Jeannie returned the smile. "I'm excited too. And don't worry, I brought my famous potato salad. It's a recipe that's been passed down through my family on my mother's side." Jeannie thought to herself that if the opportunity presented itself today, she would tell Ismail and his wife about Myrtle Beach and the whole step-mom, biological mom scenario.

Ismail chuckled. "Ah, the secret family recipe! I can't wait to taste it. I'll make sure the grill is ready to go while you get settled." Jeannie joined Ismail's family in the pool. The water was so nice and warm. Ismail's wife had set up tables adorned with patriotic decorations. There were colorful streamers, miniature American flags, and red, white, and blue tablecloths. The grill was sizzling, with Ismail tending to the burgers and hot dogs.

Ismail's mother, Sarah, approached Jeannie with a warm smile. "Thank you for joining us today, Jeannie. We're so grateful to have you as part of our family. You're like a second daughter."

Jeannie hugged Sarah. "Thank you for welcoming me, Sarah. It means a lot to me. I'm honored to be part of your Fourth of July celebration."

Ismail's oldest daughter, also named Sarah, was almost eighteen years-old and would graduate high school this year. A 'straight A' student, she had her heart set on becoming a surgeon. Ismail confided in Jeannie that he sure hoped she earned a scholarship since he had no way of paying her tuition, not to forget his other three children.

The younger Sarah constantly stayed by Jeannie, who she had once claimed as her older sister. Jeannie loved the fact that she felt comfortable talking to her about delicate matters she was not comfortable talking about with her mom. Yet, Jeannie knew that Ismail's wife was aware that their oldest child was a grown woman.

As the day went on, friends and relatives arrived, bringing their own contributions to the feast. The air was filled with laughter, conversation, and the mouthwatering aroma of grilled delicacies. Jeannie's potato salad was a hit, with many guests going back for seconds and asking for the closely guarded recipe.

Throughout the day, Jeannie couldn't help but feel grateful for the love and acceptance she had found with Ismail's family. Despite not being connected by blood, they had embraced her as one of their own. And as they gathered to celebrate Independence Day, Jeannie couldn't help but reflect on the freedom and love she had found in her new family.

As the sun began to set, Ismail's father, Michael, eighty-one years young, gathered everyone for a heartfelt speech about the importance of unity and celebrating diversity. They ended the day by watching a spectacular fireworks display, oohing and aahing at the vibrant bursts of color that illuminated the night sky.

Jeannie's secret about her inheritance and newfound wealth would have to wait for another day.

Coming Soon...

House on Haunted Hill: Resurrection is a contemporary reimagining of the iconic Vincent Price horror film. After serving a twenty-year sentence for his wife's murder in the notorious House on Haunted Hill, Frederick Loren decides to host another haunted house party with a sinister agenda—to expose several self-proclaimed psychics as frauds. Seven individuals, each harboring their own flaws, eagerly accept Loren's invitation, enticed by the promise of a $100,000 prize if they survive the night.

Unbeknownst to the guests, the mansion's previous owner, Watson Pritchard, firmly believes in its haunted nature, and his convictions prove chillingly accurate. The malevolent spirit of Inquisitor Torquemada, along with his bloodthirsty henchmen, awakens from its slumber after years of dormancy, fixating its supernatural wrath on the unsuspecting guests.

Soon after their arrival, the guests discover the sinister truth—they are trapped inside the house until morning, with no electricity, internet, or cellphone reception. The windows are barred, and the doors are impenetrable steel. Unsettling events quickly unfold, with guests vanishing one by one in the labyrinthine corridors of the haunted house.

As the vengeful ghosts grow increasingly active, the remaining guests embark on a desperate quest to find a means of escape, all while Frederick Loren's hidden cameras capture the night's terror, intending to expose the fraudulent psychics. But as the house's sinister forces close in, survival takes precedence over unveiling the truth, and the guests must confront their deepest fears and unravel the secrets that bind them to the *House on Haunted Hill.*

Beneath the Earth is a gripping horror/science fiction novel that combines the thrill of exploration with the terror of supernatural creatures. Set in the desolate landscape of Russia, a group of American scientists find themselves plunged into a nightmarish battle for survival when they venture into the depths of the abandoned Kola Superdeep Borehole.

When seismic activity causes the long-forgotten borehole to erupt, it releases a malevolent force into the world – gigantic, acid-spewing spiders that have lurked beneath the Earth's surface for centuries. As the creatures emerge from the depths, the Russian government urgently requests the expertise of American scientists to assess the situation and contain the growing threat.

Driven by a mix of scientific curiosity and a desire to prevent a potential global catastrophe, the team descends into uncharted darkness. Battling their way through hordes of terrifying spiders, the scientists enter the lair of these nightmarish creatures, only to stumble upon a shocking discovery.

Deep within the abandoned borehole lies a former Soviet Union top-secret laboratory where scientists were experimenting with the spiders to create a super weapon. Unleashing unintended consequences, their experiments resulted in the creation of an even larger and more terrifying creature – the queen of the spiders.

As the team unravels the dark secrets of the laboratory, tensions rise, and trust begins to waver. Each member must confront their deepest fears while fending off relentless attacks from the monstrous spiders and the colossal queen. With their lives hanging in the balance, they must find a way to escape the labyrinthine depths before they become victims of both the spiders and the deadly secrets hidden within the laboratory.

In this heart-pounding horror book, *Beneath the Earth* explores themes of isolation, the fragility of the human psyche, and the destructive consequences of tampering with nature. The relentless pursuit of knowledge clashes with the chilling reality of facing supernatural horrors, pushing the characters to their limits.

Prepare to be captivated, horrified, and left on the edge of your seat as *Beneath the Earth* invites you to witness the dark secrets that lie beneath our very feet, where battles with monstrous spiders and a showdown with a grotesque queen await.

www.ingramcontent.com/pod-product-compliance
Lightning Source LLC
Chambersburg PA
CBHW020256030826
48979CB00026B/1270/J
9798988682356